# Encounters

Also by Sumana Khan

The Revenge of Kaivalya

# Encounters

## Someone's Always Waiting

**SUMANA KHAN**

First published in India in 2015 by CinnamonTeal Publishing



ISBN 978–93–85523–18–2



Typesetting and cover design: CinnamonTeal Publishing

Canoe sketch: flaticon licensed under CC 3.0

CinnamonTeal Publishing
an imprint of Dogears Print Media Pvt. Ltd.
Plot No 16, Housing Board Colony
Gogol, Margao
Goa 403601 India
www.cinnamonteal.in

*For Amma*

# CONTENTS

# AUTHOR'S NOTE

Dear Reader,

*Encounters* is a bunch of five uneven, quirky creations. They are misfits in form and genre, inheriting this wretched trait from their creator. Does one classify them as short stories, novellas or novelettes? We shall leave the debate to the more pedantic reader. Irrespective of their classification, these are stories that found their logical conclusions.

I have skidded along the borders of paranormal and fantasy fiction genres. Even so, the crux of this work is to examine (a very feeble attempt, I assure you) the tragedy and horror inherent in human existence—loneliness, bereavement, the quest for identity, the conditional cruelty of relationships, to name a few. Yet, we not only thrive, but triumph. Our ability to love, to be loved, to rise above our situations—these are the reasons why we still exist despite our self-annihilating tendencies.

—*Sumana Khan*

The seconds hand moved by a tick and I turned thirty-two just as quietly. Thirty-two and single—that's how I'd be described. Not thirty-two and accomplished, or thirty-two and happy. Thirty-two and single. Spoken as if it were a diseased condition.

As always, I'd have to wait for nearly a month before I could have a sane conversation with my parents. Perhaps longer this time. My birthday had officially become a day of mourning for them; a reminder of their failure to perform their foremost duty—that of securing a husband for me. The day was celebrated accordingly with tears, frosty dinners and awkward conversations.

My mother had called an hour ago to wish me in advance. These before-birthday calls followed a similar template every year. The call would start with pleasantries followed by a list of weddings my parents had attended, with ages of the brides thrown in casually. Or it would be updates about someone's pregnancy; of course, the age of the new mother would be included. Then, the real conversation would start. 'We hope you will make us happy at least this year. Your father and I are not getting any younger. We want to finish our duty while our limbs are strong and agile. See from the practical point of view, Ratna. After we are gone, who will look after you? Besides, the more you delay, the more difficult it will be to conceive.'

This time, my mother was more aggressive. 'I will not tolerate any more excuses', she said, her voice cracking. 'Enough! Enough of your being alone. For how long should we wait thinking you are getting over ... you know ... whatever happened? We have one family in mind. Your father and uncles have already made discreet enquiries. This year, at any cost, I want to put *akshate* on your head. We want to see a *mangalsutra* around your neck. We have invited the boy and his family for your birthday dinner tomorrow. You better wear something nice and come on time. Make this birthday truly special for all of us.' After many other threats and requests, she hung up.

I thanked my stars that I stayed on my own. I don't think I could have withstood this pressure for a second time had I lived under their roof. Initially, these conversations would hurt like a knife drawn across a vein. After all, I was Dr Ratnaveni Madhehalli Kamat, university gold medallist, India's youngest award-winning forensic analyst, the only woman to have access to the country's most secure crime databases—and all my parents saw in me was failure.

The passing years have reduced this sharp pain to a dull throb. I've stopped struggling for their acknowledgement. That's what age does to you—it holds you by the scruff and pushes you up-close towards whatever truth you are running away from. You are forced to see the truth in all its naked ugliness. You can either shrug your shoulders, accept it and start living the Real Life. Or you can close your eyes, deny the truth and continue with your bullshit version of life moulded by 'culture', or worse, Bollywood.

My truth? My parents perceive me as an extra piece of luggage that must be given away. On account of my gender. The worst part is they don't even realise it. Sounds dramatic when I put it that way. Well, that's the festering truth. They don't see me as a functioning, complete human being. They see me as a dishonourable, incomplete entity, who must be lassoed viciously, brought back into the pen, made complete by a man and a life-role that is deemed honourable for a woman. Don't get me wrong—I'm not against marriage, nor am I a misandrist. But I'm not in a place where I can even think about a relationship, let alone marriage. Certainly not one arranged by my parents—I don't trust them anymore. They don't understand, or maybe they don't want to understand how deeply scarred I am ... from that one experience. Time cannot heal wounds inflicted on one's soul. It can reduce the pain, sure. But the wound is always there, waiting to gape open, ripping tissues, spewing blood.

The tears came. How can they not come? No birthday was complete without them. A signature of my desolation ... of a loneliness that scooped out a little of my soul every day. I was sure one day I'd wake up completely dead, yet alive.

'Vrka!' I cried, the sobs pinching my chest. 'Come to me … why won't you come anymore?' Such rib-racking cries are like a storm; they don't last long. I wiped my face with my sleeve and changed the pillow covers wet with tears and snot. I brewed a cup of coffee and snuggled under the sheets.

The last I saw of Vrka was six years ago. I'd waited almost every night in the hope of meeting him, but he was keeping his cryptic promise. I could not tell anyone about him. How could I explain I was ferociously in love with a hallucination that had haunted me—saved me—during my most difficult time? For all the outward ordinariness, my life has been strange … yes, very strange.

I suppose it all started on my eighteenth birthday. That was the day I met Vrka. In flesh and blood. At least, that's what I think. That meeting was like a match striking in my brain. It caused a flare of most extraordinary hallucinations, changing the course of my life.

I'd just recovered from a severe bout of jaundice. My illness had been quite ravaging, so much so that my parents took up a *harke*, a holy vow, to offer a special puja at our ancestral temple in Madhehalli. The date for the puja happened to coincide with my eighteenth birthday and the family astrologer prophesied the significance—that this was a rebirth. When he came to know that it was also the day of the annual ratha yatra festival at Madhehalli, he puffed up with greater prophesies. He squinted at my horoscope and the *panchanga*. Aha! He had not paid attention to Venus sitting in Saturn's house, and Jupiter doing funny things nearby. Now it was all clear. It meant I would achieve success beyond mortal dreams—no, I would not be the first woman on Mars, but I would marry and settle down in a foreign land and travel all over the world with my husband. As if that weren't enough, I'd also pop out not one or two, but three babies. The elders of my family were so happy upon hearing this destiny that they decided to host the entire ratha yatra.

Madhehalli is about a three-hour drive from Bengaluru. We set off at five in the morning in a twenty-seater van. There were fifteen of us; my parents, three uncles (elder brothers to my father), their wives and six cousins—three boys and three girls. The boys also had turned eighteen that year; the girls were thirteen–fourteen.

The whole family stayed on the same street, and even though we did not live under the same roof, we were practically a joint family. We have a very successful family-run silk export business. It was a given that the boys would join the business. The girls would marry well.

The route to Madhehalli is via Tumkur. About twenty kilometres after Tumkur, an almost indiscernible road forks off towards Madhehalli. This last fifteen-kilometre stretch has always been my favourite part during Madhehalli trips. The road is almost always deserted and has a tinge of wilderness, thanks to the surrounding forests. It had been tarred a decade ago, but the red soil of the area had reclaimed the tarred surface.

It was nearing seven when we turned into this road. The silence of the place overpowered the growl of our engine. It was hard to believe that we were a few minutes away from a bustling city. Of the myriad bird calls, I could only identify the woodpecker and the koel.

Midway, we stopped by the side of the road for breakfast. My mother and aunts had packed idlis and *upma*. Flasks of filter coffee were passed around. I ate very little, and even though my tongue was parched, I barely wet my lips with water. Given a choice between a bursting bladder and a parched tongue, I'd gladly suffer the latter. There was no way I'd go pee behind a tree or a shrub.

Breakfast was done. Used paper plates and cups were packed in plastic carry bags and flung inside the forest. I protested but was quickly shushed. 'We can't carry such dirty plates touched by our spit inside the village today', Pramila aunty had scolded. She was the eldest daughter-in-law of the family. Boisterous, always meant well ... irritating most times.

Everyone dispersed to pee—the women going off in one group, the men having an ample choice of trees. I sat on a rock by the side of the road, deeply breathing in the forest air, my face upturned to the warm sunlight. How nice it would be, I thought, to just walk away. Never to be found again. No exams, no degrees, no expectations. I imagined walking away into the forest. Deep, deep into the forest. What would they do? They'd search for me up and down the road. Then they'd call the police. A search party, maybe the CRPF, would enter the forest. But I would never be found. No, I would hide ... my reverie was cut short when my mother screamed, *'Aiyoo devre!* RATNA!'

My eyes snapped open and I stood up, swaying with a severe head rush. Something has happened to Amma, I thought. It was only then that I noticed it. The wolf. Standing just three feet away from me. Staring at me with those amber eyes, made all the more hypnotic by the perfect black pupils. Nothing about its stance was threatening, not that I knew anything about wolves.

Hearing my mother's screams the men came running. They too stopped short when they saw the wolf. I heard my father say, 'Putti, don't make any sudden moves. We will try and distract it.'

But I felt faint—what if I flopped to the ground right in front of the wolf? I slowly seated myself back on the rock, never breaking eye contact with the beast. It was so strange; the wolf seemed unperturbed by all the people surrounding it. We continued to stare at each other. The men took out our steel tiffin *dabbas* and beat them against the van and the ground. The wolf, oblivious to the clanging cacophony, continued to stare at me. One of my idiotic cousins took a stone and threw it at the animal before anyone could stop him. A guttural growl filled the air as the wolf barred its serrated teeth and turned to stare at the men.

'No!' I screamed. The growl stopped immediately. The wolf looked at me one last time and slunk away into the forest. I trembled with exhaustion. I was almost lifted into the van and everyone tumbled in. We sped off even before the doors were slammed shut.

My mother was in tears. Everyone discussed the strange behaviour of the wolf. By the time we reached Madhehalli, it was concluded that 'someone had done something against me'. It was black magic, for sure. How much more should my child suffer, my mother wailed. Even the jaundice was not a 'by chance' affliction, it was deduced. Yes, someone was insanely jealous of me—of my so-called beauty, of my second rank in SSLC, of my tenth rank in PUC II, of my future NRI husband and my future kids (three in number, mind you). Meanwhile, I was racking my brain about predator behaviour. Was the wolf marking its prey? All I knew was wolves hunted in packs, and predators that hunt in packs usually have a very strategic game plan to get their quarry. I shuddered.

We reached Madhehalli in an hour. The temple, dedicated to Lord Narasimha, is situated on the outskirts of the village and can be reached only by foot. The path to the temple takes us along the banks of a tributary of Veera Vaishnavi river. On an ordinary day, the sandy banks are a great picnic spot. We'd often have lunch by the riverside, and while the elders snoozed, we kids would walk around collecting shells buried in the sand.

But today, it was like kumbh mela. It looked like the entire Tumkur district had turned up for the rath yatra. Many people were taking bath in the river, doing the mandatory three dips and praying to the sun. Colourful sarees, towels and shirts were spread on the banks to dry. Make-shift stalls had sprung up, selling freshly fried condiments and snacks.

As we walked in twos and threes, many in the crowd recognised us and greeted us. We were, after all, the 'temple family'. I walked next to my mother, smiling at familiar faces. A few of the women in the crowd called out to me, 'Ratnamma, you have grown so tall. We must find you a husband now.' Yes, that was a good reason to get married, I thought, I'd reached the right height. But they meant well, those women, and I promised myself not to be needlessly cynical.

The walk was slow, we were weaving in and out of the milling devotees. My mother stopped to buy jasmine garlands and I stood next to her, looking around. I loved to buy knick-knacks in these village fairs; last time I'd bought a handcrafted jewellery box. It had a pattern of jasmine and roses carved all over. The finishing was rough and tacky, but what could one get for thirty rupees these days? It was carved by a leathery seventy-year-old man with a patch on one eye. The box was made of jungle wood and varnished with rosewood stain. Red velvet paper lined the inside of the box. I gave the one-eyed man a fifty-rupee note and asked him to keep the change. He would hear none of it. So he wrapped two dozen green glass bangles in a newspaper and kept that in the box. 'Wear it on your wedding day', he commanded. I have preserved his gift and the box carefully. I hoped to buy something equally interesting this time.

Just as I was looking around, my eyes fell on a man quite ahead on the road. His back was turned to me, but he seemed like a foreigner. He was quite tall and walked slowly, turning his head this way and that as if walking in an arts museum. I was amused to see that he stopped after every couple of paces and with his face upturned to the sun, he breathed in deeply like an animal catching a scent. His dirty blonde hair took on a coppery tinge in the morning sun and fell about his shoulders in a wiry mess. One of those tourists in quest of exotic India, I thought. Of all the places, he had alighted at Madhehalli. But it did look like the locals knew him—unlike other places, no one stared and gawked at him; no one pestered him to buy things; no kids tried to wheedle stuff out of him. What brought you here, stranger? I thought.

He turned around purposefully, slowly, as if someone had spoken to him, and looked directly at me. My hand went up to my mouth to stifle the scream that welled up. I distinctly remember the strain on my eyelids as I opened them wide in a fear reflex. The man had the face of the wolf.

I don't remember fainting, but I apparently fell face down on the jasmine baskets. I was put on a vegetable cart and ferried to the temple. I revived when we reached the temple and looked around in panic. There was no sign of the tall man.

'Here, putti. Have some tender coconut water', my mother shoved a straw into a chopped tender coconut and gave it to me. I pushed it away, although I wanted to have it in one big slurp. There were no toilets nearby that I could use—even the priest's house was far off. So, drinking any kind of liquid was out of question.

My mother got irritated. 'Don't be stubborn like this', she said. 'Otherwise we will have to take you to a hospital and put you on IV drips.'

'My stomach is not okay', I whispered tearfully, untruthfully. 'I don't want to vomit, or worse, feel the need for the other thing.'

'Okay, okay', my mother patted my head. She and my father conferred with the priest about a safe place for me to rest while they attended the ratha yatra.

The priest pointed to a stone mandap on a small hillock behind the temple. The hillock was all boulders with tufts of grass and purple wild flowers growing from beneath the rocks.

'Let us put her there', the priest said. 'It will get very hot towards noon. It will be cool under that mandap. Of course, she can sit here in the temple too. But from the mandap, she can at least see the ratha yatra. After all, you are doing the puja in her name only no?'

My mother insisted on staying with me, but I would have none of it. 'I'll be perfectly fine. You finish the puja and come back. If I feel tired, I can always lie down.' My cousin Mohan left a jute bag with me. 'It has water and some fruits, putti ... in case you feel thirsty and hungry.'

The mandap was very rudimentary—it had six stone pillars holding up a couple of large stone slabs as the roof. Going by the carving on the pillars, it was evident that this structure too was as old as the temple. I wondered about its purpose—it was hardly four feet by four. Perhaps some yogis sat here in meditation?

I sat against one of the pillars and viewed the scene below. I had a 360-degree view of Madhehalli and the surrounding areas. As far as the eye could see, the earth was lush with paddy fields and coconut palm estates. Hidden behind the hillock, away from the sight of the temple, there was a large pond. I imagined the priest in the old days, walking all the way around the hillock to fetch water from this pond for the temple. One copper pot on the head, one on the waist. Today, there was a borewell in the temple premises, and the priest had it relatively easy.

The yatra started a little before noon. The sun was merciless and I could feel the heat radiated by the boulders. Despite the still air, wafts of agarbatti and camphor fragrance reached me even at this height. The chanting and the bhajans were but a murmur. I was glad to sit under this cool stone shelter; down there, with all the pushing and shoving bodies, I'd have fainted again.

I guess I had dozed off because the silence woke me up. I could not hear the crowd at all. I sat up in panic, staring at the empty streets below. Somewhere far off, bouncing between the cawing of crows, I heard a faint clash of cymbals. I squinted and looked at the horizon. The sun was a blinding white disc on a bleached sky and I could barely open my eyes. I saw a saffron flash of the holy *dwaja* or the flag; the chariot had moved to the far end of the village. It would probably take another forty-five minutes for the procession to return to the temple.

I felt faint again and my vision blurred. There was a sickly bitterness in my mouth; my lips felt dry and stuck together; my tongue felt like Velcro. I was dehydrated for sure–I'd not had a sip of water for more than six hours. Serves you right for lying to your mother ... that too in a temple, I chastised myself. I opened the bag that Mohan had left behind and was dismayed to see only clothes—towels, extra sarees and *veshtis*. He had left behind the wrong bag. This meant the bag with water and fruits was in the car, parked more than two kilometres away. I rummaged through the bag again, tears blurring my vision, hoping to find something, even a chewing gum, but there was nothing.

I was now in a frenzied state of panic, and that increased my dizziness. The only option I had was to go to the temple and get to the borewell inside the premises. I looked at the blazing rocks, the million steps I had to descend. Would I be able to make it? What if I fell unconscious on the way down? I'd probably hit one of those boulders and my skull would split open like a coconut. My brains would plop out and sizzle on the hot stones like an omelette. I cursed my overactive imagination.

I turned around and looked at the pond. That was a more gentle descent. I was sure the pond water was not fit for drinking. But I had to get some fluid inside me. In fact, there was a good chance of finding some people near the pond, maybe women washing clothes or kids taking a swim. I could ask them for help.

I stood up unsteadily, holding one of the pillars for support. I waited for the dizziness to pass and stepped out in the sun. The infernal heat immediately ignited a headache, and I saw pulsing lights in front of my eyes. My silk and chiffon salwar kameez crackled with static and instantly stuck to my skin. I cursed Pramila aunty—I'd worn a simple cotton salwar kameez, but no. Pramila aunty said it was my birthday and this was a temple function and I had to wear 'something nice'. I felt as if I was wrapped in cling film. Sweat collected below my armpits and spread in sickly wetness. My hair, my damned waist-length hair, acted as a heat insulator, trapping all the sunrays and setting my head on fire. It was a good thing I had disobeyed Pramila aunty at least on this count and had plaited my hair. Pramila aunty wanted me to 'leave the hair free like Deepika Padukone in that coconut oil advertisement'. She had further lamented that 'single plait makes you look very old and serious and not at all modern'. Well, despite the single plait hanging like a cow's tail from the nape of my neck, I felt my brains were being pressure-cooked inside the cranium—such was the heat of that afternoon. This is the last puja I'd ever attend, I thought angrily as I made my way towards the pond.

I was halfway down the slope when I stopped short. The wolf was back. It was crouching on the bank opposite to the hillock and lapping up water. Even at this distance I could see its long, pink tongue flicking in and out, in and out. There was no way I'd get to the pond now. I turned around, dismayed at the incline I had to work against. I must have made some noise; the wolf's ears prickled and turned, and the beast lifted its head from the water slowly, its muzzle still dripping. It ran its tongue over its muzzle and seemed to look right at me. It stood and stretched languidly. Then, causing barely a ripple, it began to swim across the pond, towards the hillock.

Adrenaline kicked in and I began to ascend the slope in great speed, or at least what I thought was great speed. I heard panting; there was no way I could tell if that was the wolf behind me or my own gasps. Then, to my horror, I could actually feel my brain switch off—I had used up every last reserve of my energy. I did not even make it to the mandap. I swayed for a foothold as a bleak message from my dying brain urged my legs to carry me forward to a nearby boulder. But my legs buckled, and I knew I was going to roll down all the way to the pond. The wolf would probably be at my throat before I hit the bottom. In that split second before I lost consciousness completely, I felt a strong pair of arms hold me.

When I came to, I realized I was being carried down the slope. I was so dehydrated that I could not even open my eyes. I had one arm around this person's neck, and my head lolled against his chest as he cradled me like a baby and jogged downwards towards the pond. 'Water', I said loudly. At least I thought I said that aloud; my lips had barely moved. I wanted to tell the man about the wolf. But I felt lethargic. It felt good—weight off my feet; my ear pressed against his chest, listening to his life rhythms.

The man had stopped walking. He gently laid me on the sandy bank, in the shade of a boulder. I heard his footsteps fade away and approach again. Then, I felt drops of water on my face; my mouth peeled open instinctively, the tongue flicking out greedily. I still could not open my eyes. I felt him rub water on my lips. I ran my tongue over my lips, like the wolf, and parted my lips again.

I was gently pulled into a seated position. He sat next to me and cradled my neck in the crook of his elbow. I felt the tip of a bottle touch my lips.

'Little sips, okay', he said.

My tongue came unstuck—water, when you are thirsty this way, is the tastiest thing in the world.

He held the bottle such that I could have only a few sips at a time. I could now open my eyes.

'Hello there', he smiled.

I could not focus on his face. I saw only flashes; my eyeballs kept sliding up and my eyelids kept shutting. I did register that he was the foreigner I'd seen earlier. He did not have a wolf-face. He had a mole on his neck.

I now felt a straw on my lips—probably a Fruity from a tetra pack.

'Slow sips, okay?' he said.

I felt more revived and slightly stronger. Gone was the dizziness. I tried to sit up.

'Easy, easy', he said, gently guiding me to lean against the boulder. He sat cross-legged in front of me. A backpack lay unzipped next to me.

'Your dehydration was quite alarming', he said. He was lean in a wiry way, and I could see nerves snake up on his arms and disappear under his sleeves. He was in a faded blue cotton t-shirt and khaki shorts. He fished out a packet of potato wafers from his backpack.

'We need to replace salt and sugar in your body. Here, have these wafers. Take sips of juice in between, okay?'

I nodded. He had pale, pale eyes with flecks of gold dust in that gray. His pupils were pinpricks.

'I was sitting on the bank there', he pointed to a spot on the opposite bank where I'd seen the wolf. I could not place his accent—not that I was an expert. He was neither American nor British, for sure. More like central Europe perhaps. Or maybe one of those Scandinavian countries.

'I saw you come down the slope, and I knew something was wrong—you were stumbling across. Got to you at the right moment', he smiled. The corners of his eyes folded. His laugh lines were deep.

I smiled weakly. 'Thank you.' It came out in a raspy whisper.

'Give me a minute', he said. He wet a towel in the pond and came back. 'I'm going to squeeze some water on your head, okay? It'll bring down your body temperature.'

It was a miracle that the water did not evaporate the minute it touched my scalp. I imagined my head steaming like one of those hot water springs. How exhilarating it must feel to just dive into the pond, I thought.

'Here', he handed over the wet towel. 'Keep it on your forehead for a bit.'

'I saw a wolf', I said, following his instructions.

'You saw a what?'

'Wolf.'

He threw his head back and laughed. The laugh lines touched his eyes. 'That was no wolf. It was the Alsatian. It belongs to the temple I guess.'

'Oh. Who are you? I mean ... I'm sorry. I did not mean to be rude.'

'I'm Vrka', he smiled. 'That's v-r-k-a. I'm just your average timeless, gypsy tourist', he said with a mock bow. 'Enough of the wafers', he rummaged his backpack again. 'Ah! This is the best', he said, handing me a banana.

I ate hungrily. 'I'm sorry', I said. I was embarrassed ... no ... ashamed. First the fainting; then ... I bet I was stinking in this stupid salwar kameez, and now, I was gobbling up his food.

We heard the din of the ratha procession. It was probably coming back towards the temple. I felt a tinge of disappointment.

'If you are feeling okay, I can take you back to the temple. We can walk along the bank ... should take fifteen minutes. Half an hour if I have to carry you.'

Despite my embarrassment, I laughed. 'I think I can manage.'

'You come to India often?' I asked as we walked.

'Yes.'

'How come you came here?'

'I hitched a ride on a truck. The truck came this far. To my luck, I came across the fair here. Unplanned travel has the best surprises.'

That's a freedom I'll never taste, I thought. I wished I could walk with him some more. But we had reached a bend and the temple was right across. The ratha was just down the road.

'Well, I'll take your leave', he said.

'Oh. Won't you join the procession? It ... it will be interesting ...'

'I have a long way to go. Besides, your Lord Narasimha and I are old friends ... he'll understand', he winked.

'Wow! I'm impressed', I laughed.

'You take care of yourself now.'

'I ... what you did for me ... thank you. Really. Thank you so much.'

'And by what name shall I remember you?' he asked.

'Ratna.'

'Aha! Unplanned travel and surprises ... see? I found a gem today', he said, mirth sparkling in his eyes.

I laughed and felt warmth spread in my cheeks that had nothing to do with the scorching sun. He's no stranger to India, I thought ... after all, he knew the meaning of my name.

'I guess your folks are calling you', he pointed beyond me.

I turned around. Indeed my father was beckoning me. I turned back to say one last goodbye, but he was gone. I looked up and down the bank, but he'd vanished like a blurry dream. I walked reluctantly towards the procession. Something had shifted inside me.

I did not tell anyone about my dehydration, or of my mystery rescuer. The first few days after the visit to Madhehalli were a torment. Vrka kept buzzing in my head like a fly beating against a windowpane. It was a good thing my exams were done—I'd have surely failed. I could not hold my end of the conversation with anyone. I'd zone out, thinking, 'Which river are you following today, Vrka?'

My parents thought my listlessness was an after-effect of the jaundice and the stress of the Madhehalli trip. One night, I lay awake thinking, 'Where are you now?' I imagined Vrka sleeping under the stars; his backpack as a pillow; the wet grass prickling his skin. I replayed my dehydration again and again. My hand around his neck. His steady yet fast breaths as he carried me down the slope. His heartbeats in my ear. I imagined scenarios where I'd suddenly bump into him. In those dream sequences, I was a different person. I was wild, carefree and unpredictable. Vrka would fall helplessly in love with me. He'd ask me if I wanted to hitchhike to Binsar at the foothills of Himalayas. And that's that. Vrka and I would live life this way—hitchhiking to every nook and cranny of the earth—making love to the roar of the oceans or to the whistle of mountain winds.

'Do you think of me?' I whispered like an idiot and did not even realise I was crying. My mother chose exactly that moment to walk in.

Needless to say, there was quite a fuss. She called my father and there was some more fuss. Why was I crying? Was my head hurting? Was it my stomach? Was it something that Pramila aunty had said? I finally told them I'm nervous about my CET exam results. That assured them of my normalcy. 'Even if you want to sit at home, don't worry.'

Eventually, like all fevers, this Vrka one subsided too. I was relieved actually—such a bliss to read the newspaper or watch a boring documentary without a riot going on inside the head. It was ridiculous—I had become like those women in the novels that my cousin Isha read surreptitiously. The novels had titles like Entwined Breaths; the covers invariably featuring bare-chested men or buxom women in lingerie. Anyway, a new worry had taken over now. I was keen on pursuing a degree in medicine. But I knew that I'd never be sent out of Bengaluru for my studies. 'The only time you'll step out of this house and stay away from us is when you have a husband by your side', I was told often.

The competition to get a seat in Bengaluru colleges was intense; I was not sure if I'd score that well. My fears came true. I'd scored well enough to get a medical seat, but only in Tumkur or Davangere. Not even in Mysore. My disappointment felt like a punch in the gut.

'Why are you sitting like this? Like you have failed?' My mother chided. 'Your marks are really good. Be proud of that.'

'Yes', my father agreed. 'Take my advice. Do your engineering.

You will get in the top colleges of Bengaluru. Why, they will roll out the carpet for you. You can get a job also faster. See if you settle in the USA ... and your future husband is always travelling, till you have kids, you can have a job no?' My family was liberal that way. They encouraged us girls to work ... as long as it was convenient for everyone else.

'More than anything', Pramila aunty chipped in, 'this becoming a doctor-geector is a headache. MBBS has no value. You have to do MD. Then they will put you in some village where you will give polio drops. That's all. For this, you will be studying till you are thirty. In between if we find a good match for you and you have to leave the country, then this will be waste only.' She stopped long enough to survey her audience. Buoyed by the nodding heads of my parents, Pramila aunty drew another lengthy breath and continued, 'Just do B.E., putti. Why even B.E.? Do B.A. only—by god's grace you don't have to work for money. You are young— be jolly instead of taking so much stress. Already you are serious about everything.'

To alleviate my sadness, I was taken to watch a movie about an angry policeman who bent electric poles in frustration. I pretended that my mood was restored, lest I be subjected to more such atrocities. That night, as I lay in my bed, I felt so alone, so disconnected from my family. Not once had anyone tried to understand how important this was to me. But I was not surprised. I had learnt to accept this passive side-lining from a very young age. I had also learnt to be resourceful—to make the best movements possible with my shackles on. Yes, I could probably throw a fit, take up a seat in Tumkur. I would not be allowed to stay in a hostel for sure. My father would make several trips to Tumkur and rent a house for me. My mother would come and stay with me; living alone was out of question as far as they were concerned. Every weekend, there'd be Bengaluru–Tumkur travel. My parents would do all this with that tragic look—the one that said how dutiful we are; what sacrifices we are making for our daughter. Just thinking about it made my BP shoot up.

More importantly, Pramila aunty was right. The marriage pressure would start in a couple of years, and that was something I was dreading. It would be heartbreaking to leave my course midway to get married. I know the kind of brutal pressure my family could exert; I'd seen it with my cousin Lata. I felt exhausted just thinking about all this. This kind of loneliness in the midst of your family ... well, it crushes you from within. It's a loneliness that springs from the realisation that you are, and will always be, an extra baggage—first for your parents, then to your husband. I cried myself to sleep.

I woke up hours later to find Vrka sitting cross-legged at my feet, staring at me. 'You are not alone', he whispered, and I really woke up. I sat up, heart thudding, fumbling for the bedside lamp switch. Of course there was no Vrka. It took a long time for the echo of his whisper to subside in my head. I finally fell asleep in the wee hours of the morning. When I woke up, I had a plan.

My father was surprised when I asked him to sign an application form. 'This is for Vidhyasagar College. It is for B.Sc. in Mircobiology. I have filled up everything ... I only need your signature.'

'Sit down, Ratna', he said. 'What is this? After scoring so well, why are you going for B.Sc.?' In terms of pecking order, B.Sc. was second class. There was prestige in doing a professional course— engineering or medicine. B.Sc. meant you were the chaff that was filtered out.

My mother was setting the dining table for breakfast when she heard this. She came and sat next to me. 'Yes, why are you doing this? Do B.E. instead.'

I looked at the two of them and said, 'You know how passionate I am about medicine. But I have considered all my options carefully and have decided it is not possible for me to pursue it. This is the next best thing for me. I want to graduate in Microbiology, take up a masters in genetic engineering ... and who knows', I shrugged, 'sometime in the future, I can go for my Ph.D.'

My parents looked at each other but were silent. I suppose there was a tiny hope inside me—a merest flicker—that after hearing my plan, my parents would feel so bad they'd allow me to go to Tumkur to study medicine.

'Also, this college is just two streets away', I continued. 'If I trip at our doorstep, I will stumble into the college ... it is so near. This option is convenient from all respects ... for all of us. More importantly, it is an all-girls college', I could almost feel the air thinning from the weight of my parents' relief. That weight also crushed my fragile hope.

'What you say is true', my mother warmed up to my idea. 'Even for B.E., the colleges are so far, and I keep hearing all these stories about ragging ...'

'It is my good karma I have such an understanding daughter like you', my father said, signing my application form with a flourish. 'Any other kid would have arm-twisted her parents ... but you have always paid heed to our words, my dear.'

Well, it was time to put forth my bargaining chip. 'My only request is please allow me to finish my masters. Without that, all my hard work will be wasted', I said in a low voice.

'Of course, you don't have to tell us', my father patted my head. 'I know you are thinking of Lata—but that was a different case. Appanna came to know that some boy in her college was after her. Lata did not know about it—but why give scope for any scandal?'

Lata got married two months before her final exams—she was doing her M.E. She never finished it. Everyone said she is now 'well-settled'—husband is an investment banker; two kids; two cars; three homes (two in Bengaluru, one holiday home in Goa). As far as I was concerned, she had withdrawn into a shell. Lata had always been so vivacious, quick-witted, quick to laugh. She was like a piece of wood now. But everyone said her 'childishness' has disappeared and she was a responsible woman now. Once, I'd asked her why she never picked up her masters again. The kids were in school and she was relatively free. 'What use is an education that does not give me personal freedom?' she had muttered, before adding quickly, 'I have nothing to complain about.'

Anyway, I'd bought five years' time—that was a huge victory for me. But, time is a non-existent dimension when you love what you do. Those five uninterrupted years must have leaked through the space between my eye and the microscope. Or maybe, every time I turned a page, it must have slipped away silently like satin through fingers. How else can I explain the rush of bewilderment I'd felt, as I received the university gold medal from the governor of Karnataka? Five years—a solid block of time—had become a memory.

Vrka visited me now and then, mostly on the nights when I'd almost passed out of exhaustion. I'd wake up in my dream to see him sitting at my feet. I found it amusing—this recurring dream of mine. I was like one of those nerdy kids with no friends, so they made up imaginary friends. Every night, I'd go to sleep looking forward to 'meeting' him. It gave me a strange sense of security. It also made me aware that I'd probably see a shrink before long.

I had a couple of job offers—the most interesting one paid the least, in keeping with the laws of irony.

'Maybe you can hold off your applications for a few weeks?' my father said one evening, while dipping a Glucose biscuit in his tea. He looked at my mother.

I knew what was coming.

'We have seen this boy', my mother said. 'We are not forcing you or anything ... but just meet him.'

'We know your future aspirations so we have discussed all this in detail with his family', my father said quickly. 'In fact, I personally met him over coffee and spoke to him. His name is Surya. He has a masters in some shares or stocks or something. In fact, his entire family is very well qualified. They were very happy to know of your gold medal and Ph.D. dreams.'

'Yes', my mother continued, 'this is perfect match if you ask me. You won't even feel you've moved to another family.'

There was really nothing much to say. I was to meet the guy and his parents the next day. That night, Vrka sat next to me, my ear pressed against his thudding chest.

I can't remember much of that week, except for a constant feeling of bewilderment. It was as if I was standing on a railway platform, and some kind of a bullet train had whizzed by sucking me in through its doors. It was not a train I wanted to get on; it wouldn't take me to my destination.

I'd barely spoken to Surya. He was twenty-nine, and, as my father put it, 'a high achiever'. He had co-founded some kind of a technology company; this had been taken over by another giant technology firm; he had gotten richer than he already was.

My first meeting with him was on our terrace. We spoke briefly of our interests—he, mostly of his business vision; me, about DNA and molecules. He was based out of Florida, but he travelled most of the time. He went hiking, swimming, mountaineering, played baseball and tennis and when 'there's really nothing to do', it was just 'chillax with Grand Theft Auto'. So, what could I say about my hobbies? My only travels had been between pages. I did not even know what that theft auto thing was. I felt dumb in front of him. That, ironically, made me feel happy. He'd surely say no—we had absolutely nothing in common. I thought that was the end of it.

Imagine my bewilderment when my family started behaving as if I were his wife. I was, of course, alarmed. My concerns over lack of common interests were pooh-poohed. 'Those things are immaterial', my mother told me. 'What is important is his character, his family, is he able to give you a good life or not?'

I felt as if I was invalid: incapable of taking care of myself in this strange adult world, and so someone must always be my caretaker.

'What is there?' my father chipped in. 'Tomorrow he will take you also for climbing mountains. See, putti, not everyone is lucky enough to get such a perfect match like this. In every respect, I can't find a single fault with him. Not one single bad habit. I asked him directly. I told him—look, consider me as your friend and tell me, do you smoke, drink, eat red meat? He told me, "Uncle, I am very conscious of my health, so I don't smoke. As far as alcohol is concerned, I won't lie to you. I move in CEO circles, so yes, I do have the occasional wine, champagne and beer. But it is not that I drink every day." And he is a vegetarian. Where will you find such a boy?'

I did not have an answer. How could I explain that my saying no was not about finding so-called faults with him—it was just that I was not ready yet? I did not have any more bargaining chips. I was exhausted—buying time, buying freedom, buying breathing space all my life.

Four days after I'd first met Surya, his parents came home laden with gifts. Their son had said yes. There was much jubilation in my house. I felt cornered, insignificant.

I decided to talk to Surya directly. Perhaps he too was under pressure? We met at a coffee shop.

'I'm sorry', he said, 'I wanted to personally call you and tell you of my interest ... but my parents insisted I follow tradition.'

I was taken aback. 'I am very surprised', I said. 'I mean we don't have anything in common. Don't you think it's too fast?'

The waiter came with my latte and his black tea. Surya eyed

my large cup, frothing with foam and cream. 'Better watch that', he said, smiling. 'You won't fit into the wonderful wardrobe I've planned for you.'

'Sorry, what?' The blood thrummed in my ears.

He leaned forward, still smiling. 'Do you know why I'm a successful entrepreneur, Ratna?' He did not wait for a reply. 'Everyone thinks it is hard work, intelligence. Sure, it is. But there is one underlying factor. My instinct. I go by gut feel. It is a gift, if you ask me.'

I still did not know what he was getting at.

'The minute I saw you, I knew this is a done deal. I just knew you are perfect for me. I will be honest with you. I don't believe in love at first sight. I don't know if this attraction I have can be called "love" ... yet. But this I can say—this will work out perfectly. I mean, my parents made me meet three other girls. All three were entrepreneurs. I guess my parents thought that commonality will click—but it did not. Those girls were as opinionated and aggressive as I am', he laughed. 'Hey, nice to catch up with them on the cocktail circuit, but I couldn't picture myself living with them.'

I stared at my latte for a minute. This did not turn out the way I'd planned at all. I was forming words and sentences in my head; I had to tell him that I felt the same way about him, the way he felt about those other girls.

'You know it's getting noisy in here. Do you mind if I take you on a drive? We can talk peacefully', he said.

I nodded.

Soon, we were on the outskirts of Bengaluru, beyond Kanakpura. We spoke of the real estate expansion and infrastructure woes. He spoke of town planning in the various countries he'd visited. He took a detour from the main road that brought us to a mud track leading to a patch of sugarcane fields. It was nearing six in the evening. Barring the evening bird calls and the traffic murmur far off, this deserted place was cloaked in silence. A tiny alarm bell went off in my head.

'So tell me', he said, switching off the engine.

'One second', I said, dialling a number on my phone. 'I'll inform my father our whereabouts ... they'll be expecting me home any minute now.' That ought to keep him in check, I thought, in case he had any funny ideas.

Surya snatched the phone from me even before I could say hello. 'Uncle, this is Surya', he said, winking at me. 'Ratna and I came out for coffee. I brought her to a cafe near Kanakapura. We are on our way back, but the traffic is quite bad. Just wanted to let you know that I'll drop her off by seven-thirty.' He switched on the speaker and held it up with a smile.

'As long as she is with you, I have no worries, Surya', my father's voice conveyed the smile on his face. My smokescreen of security dissipated.

'There you go', Surya said, handing back my phone. 'Now you can talk all you want.'

I got out of the car, pretending that I needed to stretch my legs. He got out too. 'Lovely place', he said looking around.

'Look, Surya', I began, 'you have built your career ... your success ... with your own hands, right?'

He came around the car and stood next to me. 'Yes, of course. Did not take any help from anyone. My father pitched in with the initial funds though.'

'Forget the funds', I said, leaning against the car. 'I mean it was your effort, your blood and sweat ... it's ... it's yours. The entire journey. It's yours.' Surya was staring at me. He just nodded.

'That's what I want for my life. I have my own career plans, my own future goals ... I want to fulfil them. Just the way you have done. I have this job offer ... it's a perfect foundation for my research interest. Like you ... I want to experience this journey of ... of becoming something', I looked at him, feeling embarrassed at my outburst. 'This is going too fast for me. I want some more time to—'

Surya leaned over, cupped my chin and kissed me on my lips.

'Hey!' I flinched. Pinned to the car, I tried to push him away. I heard him chuckle, his nose pressed against my cheek, his hands now circling my waist.

'Come on, sweetie', he said, breathing into my ear. I was still trying to push him away, my hands mere twigs trying to dislodge a boulder. 'How will we ever have those prophesied three kids if you push me away?' he said laughing, kissing my neck.

I was too numb to respond.

'Sorry, I could not help it', he said with a smirk, his hands still around my waist.

Just then, we heard a rustling noise behind us, and some of the sugarcane stalks quivered. Someone was making their way towards us.

I felt sick with fear—what if it were some local men ...

The air filled with a growl—guttural, grating, rabid.

'Shit! Get in the car!' Surya yelled.

The growl turned into a deathly howl as we sped towards the main road.

I almost burst into tears as we joined the traffic. Relief and disgust flooded me. Surya had uncontrollable fits of laughter. 'What the hell was that? Some rabid dog was jealous of my kiss', he winked.

I remained silent. I felt belittled and angry. More than that, I could taste fear—leaden and crusty—in my mouth.

That night, after dinner, I decided to talk to my mother.

'Where is Appa?' I asked casually. 'I want to talk ... only to you.'

'He is downstairs watching T.V. What happened?'

We were sitting on my bed, sorting the laundry.

'There's something I don't feel right about ... about this whole alliance', I said softly.

My mother folded and unfolded a towel a couple of times, without saying anything for a few moments. Then she said, 'Look, putti, it is okay to be scared. Every girl feels scared about marriage. We have brought you up like a crystal doll; made sure nothing ever hurt you; gave you all the comforts. Likewise, you have also kept our honour. Now all of a sudden, you are going into this stranger's house—far away from all of us. It is okay to be scared.'

'It's not ... not that', I said. My heart was hammering—how do I tell her about what happened? But I narrated the whole thing without taking a breath. I told her how I felt intimidated when he stopped at a deserted place. I told her about feeling helpless, insulted, when he kissed me without my consent.

'You are so innocent; really you are only a child in a woman's body, putti', my mother smiled. 'Of course, this happened. He loves you. You are a woman on the threshold of marriage now.

These are all private things between you and your husband. You should never discuss this with anyone, okay?' She patted my head and left.

I was stunned by her reaction. Did I not explain properly? All these years, they wouldn't even allow me to go out alone to a salon or a nearby shop; I always had to be shepherded by someone—my mother, aunt or cousins. Now, a stranger comes on the scene, and they hold me out—this exquisite crystal doll, as they see me—and tell him, 'Here, you may play with this doll.'

A sense of betrayal and self-loathing squeezed my heart. Ten days ago, I did not even know of this guy's existence. Even now, apart from his work and his so-called hobbies, what did I know about him? What did he know about me for that matter? We were strangers for all practical purposes. Yet, this stranger thought it was perfectly okay to kiss me, touch me, despite knowing I was not for it. He came with an entitlement to behave this way with me because everyone had given him the sanction. Everyone but me. So what was my value in my own life ... in anyone's life? What was this innocence they accused me of? Do they really believe I don't understand passion, lust, sex?

I fell asleep exhausted. I was back at the hillock at Madhehalli that night, naked and terrified. Only, there was no pond, no temple, no Madhehalli. I was abandoned on the stone mandap, and whenever the moon floated out of the clouds, I could see there was no way out of the mandap—the hill fell off in steep cliffs on all sides. The ravines below were moving, slithering, hissing. Hideous serpents—fangs barred, hoods spread—waited for me to fall into their midst. How their evil eyes twinkled like burning coal embers! Even in the moonlight, I could see their forked tongues flicking in and out in frenzy, having scented my animal fear. Then, to my horror, a couple of serpents had reached the mandap. They slithered purposefully towards me, their hissing mocking my helplessness, fangs glinting in the moonlight. I had no way out. I only had to choose a better death. Do I jump? Do I stand still?

I imagined taking the jump—the wind in my hair, raising goose bumps on my naked skin; my eyes wide open to take in the upturned hoods in their lusty wait, their hissing drowning out my scream. I imagined falling into their midst—their muscular bodies cushioning my fall. And then ... and then ... their cold bodies would slither all over me, their forked tongues prickling my skin, taking in the scent of my death-sweat. I could feel those writhing fiends entwine my battered body, squeezing my legs, thighs, breasts and finally my neck. That's when I would feel the million pinpricks—the venomous fangs sinking into my flesh, the injected venom roaring into my bloodstream.

I chose to stand still and get bitten by the snakes in the mandap. Yes, it was better to die a quick, writhing death here, rather than falling into their midst below. I stood still as the serpents curled at my feet, hoods spread, ready to strike. And then ... I was lifted in the air. The serpents fell away, hissing angrily. It was him! Vrka! Vrka!

I was back in my room, safe, ensconced in his arms, weeping bitterly. 'You are always safe with me', he said, stroking my hair, rocking me to and fro. I woke up, still feeling his warmth around me; his voice in my ears. I'd slept with the lights on. Of course the room was empty. I'd just had the worst nightmare of my life.

I realised I'd indeed been crying. I washed my face and switched off the light. An incredible sadness flowed in my veins like ice water and I shivered in its wake. My own parents had broken my trust in the worst possible way. They thought they sought my happiness, but it was only their happiness that counted in the end—their status, their prestige. They were supposed to be my safety net, yet they had denied me my right to dignity. No wonder I was losing my mental balance day by day. My life, I realised, had always been about negotiations, even for simple things such as watching a movie with friends or going on a college picnic. I'd learnt early enough to accept denials—no picnics, no movies with friends, not even going alone to the beauty parlour. Everything came with a caveat. No wonder my severely bruised mind was grappling for any form of crutch to balance itself, and it clung on to Vrka—a stranger who had treated me with much kindness and respect. It seemed that the only thing holding me back from a complete mental breakdown was this sliver of my imagination. I sent a silent prayer to Vrka. 'I'll probably never see you ever in my life', I whispered. 'But I want you to know, in a strange way you give me strength. For that, I love you. Yes, I love you even if you are just my imagination.' I finally drifted off to a delirious sleep.

I woke up feeling refreshed. I decided to take up the job offer.

From now on, the world could rearrange its schedule around my priorities. I lied about going to the college for some paperwork and managed to meet the CTO of the start-up. He said they were shifting to new premises with better lab infrastructure. I could come on board in two months' time. The work would centre around DNA quantitation techniques. They'd post my offer letter in a week's time.

When I returned home, flushed with this small rebellious victory of mine, I was surprised to see my entire family in a celebratory mood. They were gathered in the living room, passing around ladoos and jalebis. As soon as I entered, Pramila aunty squealed, 'Here comes the princess!'

I was soon dragged to the sofa; someone's hand put a ladoo in my mouth. Someone else placed a card on my lap. It took a few seconds for me to realise it was my wedding card. My condemnation was wrapped in red silk and embossed with glittery stones. I was to be married in three weeks' time.

'Go to the terrace', Pramila aunty said with irritating glee.

'Why? What's—'

'Go on, putti', my father urged.

As I walked towards the stairs that led to the terrace, Pramila aunty called out, 'I will come exactly in fifteen minutes with coffee.' To which one of my cousins said, 'At least give them half an hour.' Squeals of laughter stabbed my ears.

Of course, I knew the 'surprise' that awaited me. I felt the blackest of dismay on seeing Surya's face. Everything about him irritated me—he sat on my favourite chair next to the swaying palms; legs crossed, so the trousers just about revealed a ridiculous, and therefore fashionable, pair of striped socks; metal-framed sunglasses shaded the holes in his soul; his fingers were busy rubbing and tapping the screen of a phone. Imagine if you were the surprise, Vrka, I thought, my eyes brimming immediately.

'There she comes', he said standing up, taking off his silly sunglasses and placing them carefully in a case that was attached to his belt. 'I'm leaving for Bandipur with my friends. Wanted to meet you before I left', he said.

I did not reply.

'I'll be gone for a week. We hope to spot a tiger at least this time.'

'Was the wedding date discussed with you?'

'Yes. Your parents had selected a date that was nearly eight months away. I'd have said yes too ... but after yesterday ... ' he winked at me.

'Well, I guess I'll have to push the date ahead. I'm not ready to get married this early.'

He laughed. 'You know, when my parents showed your photo, I had decided this won't work. But when I saw you—your demureness, your nervousness, your ... ', he lowered his voice, 'your inexperience—it was a huge turn on for me. Don't tell me you did not enjoy yesterday.'

'I was disgusted', I said. 'Still am.'

He behaved as if he did not hear me. 'I'm sure there'll come a time when you can't get enough of it.'

I watched, as if in slow motion, his nostrils flare, his mouth draw back in a sneer. 'Yes', I heard myself say, 'I'm sure there'll come a time when I can't get enough of it. Only, it won't be with you.'

He mock-clapped. 'How the deer roars!' he laughed.

'Look', I said, leaning against the parapet wall, 'forget about our parents. They have a different way of looking at things. But you and me ... we belong to the same generation. First and foremost, I want my life partner to be my friend ... I want a relationship where there's mutual respect. I don't see that happening with you.'

'What do you mean?' he said, leaning in close.

I stepped away and said, 'You behaved like a pervert yesterday. I don't even feel comfortable in your presence. How much more messed up can it get? I am sorry. I will call off this marriage.'

'Hey', he said holding up his hands in mock surrender, 'I may have misjudged yesterday. But frankly, I could not help myself. You were ranting about your career and whatever, but all I could think was, "Damn she's so sexy and she does not even know it," and that makes you even more irresistible, you know?'

I was livid. 'Don't push your luck.'

'Oh oh. There she goes again. Do you know', his voice dropped, 'when you get angry like this, your face takes on a different colour ... like a ripening fruit? Your breathing becomes rapid and ... ' he stared at my breasts and grinned.

'We have to join my family downstairs for coffee', I said and started walking towards the terrace door.

'Okay, okay', he laughed and came up right behind me.

The terrace door opened into a narrow landing. The minute we were inside, Surya grabbed me by the waist and pinned me against the wall. Just as I was about to yell at him, his mouth was on mine, his tongue inside, flicking in frenzy like the serpents of my nightmare, his hissing breath scalding my cheeks, his hands crushing my breasts.

'Don't show him fear', a tiny voice said inside me. I stood still—a cold and lifeless granite statue of worship—and withstood his assault.

'I'm coming up with coffee', Pramila aunty yodelled. At that moment, her voice and footsteps were the sweetest things I'd ever heard in my life.

His tongue found its way out reluctantly, though he managed to bite my lower lip and draw blood. His hands found their way back into his pockets. My eyes did not leave his eyes. No fear, no tears, my heartbeats pulsed.

'We are on our way down, aunty', I said, my voice steel-steady. 'You will pay for this, you bastard', I hissed. Yes, like a serpent.

'I'll eagerly await your punishment', he laughed.

I rearranged my clothes, wiped my mouth with the back of my palm, turned around and walked downstairs.

He left after fifteen minutes, but not before whispering, 'I can't wait to taste you again.'

As soon as he left, my family began discussing the wedding preparations. The wedding planner was expected that evening. The venue was already booked apparently. A resort with a golf course on the outskirts of the city. Everyone agreed the invitation card was fabulous—my father would place the bulk order immediately.

I sat quietly on one of the dining chairs. I touched the spot on my lower lip where he'd bitten me. The skin was broken, tender and mushy, and it tasted blood-salty. Every time I ran my tongue over the wound, it stung and throbbed. A serpent's bite.

How did it get to this? Not once, not one bloody time did anyone in my family hear an actual YES from me. Yet, everyone had decided that I should wake up next to this beast for the rest of my life. They'd fixed the venue; they'd fixed the date; they'd picked my wedding sarees, jewellery ... everything. Was I just a pair of breasts and a womb to everyone? Well, if they thought I'd go like a cow to a slaughterhouse, they were in for a surprise.

But first, I wished there was a place I could escape to, where I could be alone, just for a while. The only option I had was to shut myself in my room. I had to ... had to heal. To figure out my next steps. There was no way this wedding could take place.

I reached the stairs leading to my room when my mother called out. 'Where are you running away, dear? Come and sit with us.'

'Yes, yes', Pramila aunty chirped. 'We know you are feeling sad that your hero has gone away for a week. But after three weeks, no one will disturb you.' Everyone tittered.

'Come; come here, dear', my mother called. 'See the invitation card again.'

The happiness on her face tore me. How I wished this had worked out. What a catastrophic grief awaited them! Even so, their grief was nothing; it would never measure up to the horror of living with that pervert; the cold, dank fear of hearing his footsteps; his breath; his voice.

I stood still, staring at them, hands limp by my side. My lower lip was beginning to swell. 'Don't', I said. 'Don't be a part of this sin. Burn that invitation card.' I turned around and ran up the stairs. I locked myself in my room and dragged my computer table to block the door. There! Now no one could get in.

I heard their footsteps, followed by the banging on the door. I heard my father's angry diatribe. Of how ungrateful I was; despite being provided with all the comforts, despite them never denying me anything, I was behaving so irrationally. Yes, all this education had spoilt me. Or maybe it was one of my friends in college—those feminist daughters-of-whores who had put some ideas in my head. 'No need to beg her', he yelled at my mother. 'Let her lie in that room without food and water. That will burn her bloody pride. If I catch any of you trying to give her anything, I'll break your legs. I have allowed too much independence in this house.'

I locked myself in the bathroom. His voice and the banging on my door died down. I pulled my lower lip and examined the wound in the mirror. It had turned a sick purple and was swelling by the minute. I looked at my face—gaunt, terrified, red veins curling around my pupils. When the weeping started, I thought my guts would emerge from my mouth and splash in a squelchy mess all over the sink.

After a while, when the sobs were still racking, but the eyes, squeezed off all the tears, remained dry, I decided to cleanse him off my body. I brushed and brushed—my teeth, tongue, lips. The wound flared angrily, igniting fresh tears, but I let it burn me. I stripped and stood under a scalding shower, vigorously rubbing my face and breasts. I walked out of the bathroom, naked, dripping wet. I managed to dry myself and put on fresh clothes.

I drew the curtains and lay curled like a foetus on my bed. 'Come to me, Vrka', I said. It came out as a mumble; my swollen lip wouldn't move. But he came immediately and I clung to him. 'Don't let go', I said, holding him tighter. But it was not close enough, not close enough. I wish I could dissolve into him, my cells rushing in his bloodstream, following the rhythms of his heart. The pain from my lips now radiated all over my body.

'I won't last long, Vrka. I don't want to last. It's useless ... utterly useless ... this life of mine. It is no life at all. I just breathe in and out, eat, shit and sleep. There is no dignity for me. No love. No respect.'

I felt Vrka's chest heave and my cheeks received his tears. I shrank into myself, like a T.V. being switched off—first the afterglow on the screen, then the horizontal line and finally a bleep ... and darkness.

When I came to, I felt no pain. I felt weightless; a luminance enveloped me and there was a tingling ecstasy all about me. Funnily enough, I could see every room in my house, as if there were no walls. I saw Pramila aunty and my mother in the kitchen, as usual. Mohan was in his room, watching porn on his computer. My father and uncles were sitting with the wedding planner. The clock shaped like a guitar in the living room announced it was eight through a series of beeps.

My eyes fell on my bed. Vrka sat next to my bruised body, stroking my hair. My lower lip had swollen to the size of a golf ball, and some kind of a hideous rash had broken out all around my mouth, turning the skin into the colour of aubergine. I looked like a rotting corpse. Seven hours I'd lain here, festering in my wounds and no one had come up to check on me? Gone was the ecstasy I'd felt, it was replaced by a black rage as throbbing as my wound. Only Vrka, my faithful Vrka, had stayed close to me. Vrka, a cord of my own imagination.

'Look what he did to me, Vrka', I said, floating around the bed, the rage flushed out by grief. Only, I could not shed tears in this ethereal form. My sobs were like a pulse of energy that dissipated my very atoms—I formed and re-formed over and over as sadness consumed me.

Maybe rage and grief have some kind of a presence, like radio wave interference. I saw my mother look up at the ceiling as she chopped carrots. I saw her lips move. 'It has been more than six hours, Pramila. Come with me ... let us feed her and talk some sense into her. She has never been this way.'

They came upstairs and knocked on the door, gentle raps at first, followed by open palm slaps. 'Open the door, putti. This stubbornness is not good.'

Pramila put her ear to the door. 'I can't hear anything inside,' she said, her voice throaty, cracked with fear.

'MOHAN!' My mother yelled. 'Get to Ratna's balcony somehow. Break open her window!'

I could see my mother's thoughts. She was imagining me swinging from the ceiling fan. My father and uncles too rushed towards my room. They threw their shoulders against the door.

Mohan had scaled down the water pipe from the terrace and had jumped onto my balcony. He used one of the wrought iron garden chairs on my balcony to break the French window glass.

'Oh my god', he screamed on seeing my body. Vrka did not look up. I floated next to Vrka, fascinated by all this activity.

Mohan moved the computer table aside and opened the door screaming, 'Call an ambulance!'

My father rushed in and held my hands to check my wrists. Yes, he thought I'd slit my wrists. Then he saw my face, hideous and swollen. I heard his thought—I must've taken some sleeping pills or drank pesticide or bleach, and the swelling was the side-effect. He put a finger below my nose, held my wrists again—no pulse, no breath.

He scooped me up. 'Get the car out. There's no time for an ambulance. It's anyway too late.'

My mother yelled, 'What do you mean it's too late? You rakshasa ... what do you mean by that? What has happened to my angel's face?' She was held back by Pramila as my father rushed downstairs cradling me.

I was so absorbed in all this, I did not notice Vrka was gone. Of course, he was gone. He was a thread of my imagination; a tongue of smoke that curled from a smouldering incense. How could he exist now that the incense had burnt out? But what was I now? Perhaps I too was just lingering smoke; soon I'd dissipate too, atom by atom into the atmosphere.

My body lay across the back seat of our sedan; my head resting on my father's lap. He stared straight ahead—unblinking, dry-eyed, yet, heart hammering. My mother sat in the front seat, weeping, as my uncle drove the car in utter panic. The rest of my family followed in another car.

The doctors worked on me furiously. I floated around, fascinated. They cut open my salwar top with a pair of scissors. Then, they cut open my bra exposing my breasts. They stuck some kind of sensors all around my left breast and rubbed a solution on my chest area. Next, they placed something on my chest and an electric surge caused my body to spasm. Even as I floated, I felt a powerful tug. There was much excitement; one of the nurses stared at a screen where a pulse jumped up and flat-lined. They did it again, and this time, the tug was even more powerful. I no longer felt weightless; I was drawn to my body; rather, I was roped in like a fish at the end of a line. With the third electric surge, I was sucked into my body in a whoosh. The roar around me was deafening; it took a moment for me to realise it was merely the sound of my own restarted heart and the ensuing rush of blood. I felt an angry rebellion well up inside me—how dare they capture me, squeeze me back into this wretched, disgusting body?

'Start IBP monitoring', the doctor's voice seemed to echo. Someone deftly stuck a needle on my artery in the elbow.

Within a minute, I heard one of the nurses yell about my rising BP. Then, I saw Vrka. Of course, now that my brain was firing again, he was back. He held my hand and kissed my forehead. 'It's not your time', he whispered, kissing both my eyes. I felt calm, safe.

The nurse announced in a perplexed tone that my BP was normal.

'Keep monitoring', the doctor instructed. 'Her BP seems unstable. How can it rise and drop so suddenly?'

I was moved to a gurney and wheeled into a ward. I heard the doctor call out to my parents. 'Only parents, please.' The doctor who saved me was a girl like me. Her parents had allowed her to fly. Mine had butchered my wings.

My parents walked in. My mother held my hand and wept.

'She is out of danger', the doctor said. 'Now that her vitals have stabilised, we will treat her septicaemia. It was life-threatening. We have taken her blood samples. But can you throw some light on what happened? What bit her?'

My father was hesitant in his reply. 'I am confused', he said eventually. 'Do you think something bit her? I thought it was an allergic reaction to ... to something she has taken.'

'No. We examined her wound. Something has bitten her. We are running toxicology tests on her blood. But if you can give some details ... any descriptions ... like, was it a spider or some insect ... we can look at specific anti-toxins.'

'I ... we don't know doctor. She went up to her room in the afternoon, and we thought she's taking rest. Maybe something bit her when she was asleep.'

The doctor left, promising to monitor me hourly. My father said, 'We must inform Surya of this accident.'

The blood roared in my ears. Vrka squeezed my hand and said, 'I'm here with you, my love. Become strong ... here and here.' He pointed to my chest and my head.

'His phone is not reachable', my father sighed.

The infection subsided considerably the next day, although there was visible swelling. I was able to speak; the words came out slurred.

'You'll be fine by tomorrow', the doctor said as she read my charts. Her name badge identified her as Dr Swarna Kumar. She was a tall and slender woman, economical in her words, precise in her actions. She radiated a no-nonsense attitude that I envied—bet Surya would not dare to touch her. I, on the other hand, was a weak, snivelling rabbit; of course, this shit had to happen to me.

'When can we get her discharged, doctor?' my mother asked. 'Her wedding is just three weeks away.'

'I will let you know by tomorrow evening. I would like to keep her under observation for a couple of days. That was a nasty infection ... we don't want a relapse.'

'What do the blood reports say? What caused this?'

'We did not find any toxins in her bloodstream. So I don't think it is any kind of insect bite or sting. Well then, I have to get on with my rounds.' The doctor left before my mother could ask any more questions.

I closed my eyes and pretended to sleep. I did not have any desire or energy to talk to my mother. I heard her call out to the nurse, 'Can you stay here for ten minutes, please? I will go to the canteen and buy some tender coconut water.'

As soon as my mother left, Dr Swarna walked into my ward. She placed a palm gently on my forehead. 'Ratna?'

I opened my eyes and looked at her.

Dr Swarna turned to the nurse and said in a low, urgent tone, 'Close the door and stand outside. Anyone comes, tell them I'm doing a regular check up. Don't allow anyone inside.'

The nurse nodded and followed the doctor's instructions.

Once the doors were closed, Dr Swarna looked at me and said, 'Ratna, I wanted to speak to you first. This wound ... it's a human bite. If this was passion gone too far ... it's your personal business. If not, this is sexual assault. I don't want to put any pressure on you. I just want you to know that if you want to take legal action, I'm there for you. The medical reports will back up your claim.'

I managed to slur, 'Ank you tho muh.'

Dr Swarna patted my head. There was kindness and strength in that touch. 'You can just nod or shake your head to my questions. Was it your fiancé?'

I nodded.

'Your parents know?'

I shook my head.

'Do you want me to tell them?'

I nodded.

'Do you want to report him?'

I thought for a couple of minutes and nodded slowly.

'Okay. We'll get you on your feet first and discuss more.'

She left but was back almost immediately with my parents, who seemed agitated. My mother was in such a hysterical state that Dr Swarna immediately administered a sedative and she was wheeled out.

I knew something was very wrong and that it had nothing to do with my injury. There was no way the doctor could have told my parents anything yet. My father sat heavily on a chair beside my bed and just kept shaking his head.

'Wha hafen?' I slurred as loudly as possible. I tried to sit up but a wave of dizziness pinned me down.

My father rushed out of the room, where he presumably encountered Dr Swarna. I heard him speak to her in a low voice. I heard Dr Swarna say, 'Yes. I will talk to Ratna. You please sit in ward 204. Your wife is resting there. I think your family is waiting in the reception area. I'm very sorry to hear all this.'

A moment later Dr Swarna walked in.

'Wha hafen dotor?'

'Ratna, there's no easy way to say it. Your fiancé is dead. I don't have any details. I'm assuming there was some kind of an accident.'

Even though I hated the guy, I felt as if I'd swallowed something unpleasant. A wave of nausea overpowered me and I dry-retched into a barf bag as Dr Swarna held me.

'I want you to speak to a counsellor, Ratna. All this is too overwhelming for you. The last thing I want you to feel is guilt.'

I was given a sponge bath after which, I slept fitfully. Vrka was back, lying next to me. He had the face of a wolf again, blood dripping from his muzzle.

Later that evening, my parents visited me. My mother had aged by two decades in the last couple of hours. My father looked lost and started pacing around.

My mother came over to me and checked my lip. 'The swelling is still there', she mumbled. Her own eyes were swollen, and her hair was in disarray.

'Well', my father said, his face contorted in fury. 'There's no hurry for her to get well now.'

'Stop talking like that', my mother pleaded.

'NO!'

I was confused—why on earth was he angry with me? I cowered at first—I was always afraid of my father's temper—but anger took over. I pulled myself up, breathing heavily with the effort.

'STOP IT!' My mother yelled and covered her ears.

'You did not want to marry, isn't it? "Burn the invitation cards" that's what you said, remember?' My father stood at the foot of my bed, snarling at me. 'Aha! What a daughter we have! What a black tongue you have for your curse to have come true!' Then he turned to my mother and said, 'We should be careful. She might have cursed us also.'

He bowed before me mockingly. 'Let me tell you how well your curse worked. You said burn the invitation cards, now his parents are running from pillar to post to burn his body. Do you know why?'

Next to me, my mother moaned and pleaded, 'Don't do this. How can she be responsible ...'

'Shut your MOUTH', my father sprayed spit.

Animal rage exploded inside me. My vision blurred, and I was seeing colourful pinpoints dancing in front of my eyes. A very tiny, rational part of my brain said that was because of a dangerous spike in my BP. I was probably very close to having a heart attack, so great was this anger that it squeezed every cell, wrung every nerve. I ripped the IV lines and sent the saline bottles crashing.

'I lay dead in my room because of that bastard', the anger had cured my slur, but my voice almost came out as a guttural growl. 'He attacked me in my own home, the safest place on earth for me. He attacked while all of you sat downstairs, laughing. He attacked because you had given him the license. Yes, while you sat downstairs feeling proud of your conquest, he pinned me to a wall, shoved his filthy tongue in my mouth, bit my lips, groped me and crushed my breasts.'

The silence in the room was thick, viscous. My left hand started tingling; my vision started fading. I was startled when Vrka rushed to me. This was the first time I'd seen him while awake. Vrka put his hand on my chest and whispered, 'Easy, my love.' He pulled me close to him and said, 'Breathe with me; breathe with me. Follow my rhythm.' The tingling stopped and my vision cleared. There was no Vrka.

My father was sitting dumbfounded at the foot of my bed.

'So', I said in a calmer tone, 'I am shocked by his death. But ... I am not sorry about it. The only thing I'm sorry about is my existence. It's worthless. I'm no more worthy than an exotic animal ... one that grows up in a beautiful cage, and when it reaches adulthood, it is exported to another beautiful cage for breeding purposes.'

My mother held me and cried.

'I did not know about this', my father almost whispered.

'I did not wish for his death', I said. 'I only wished for my escape.'

'He misbehaved with her when he had taken her out for a drive too', my mother said in between sobs. 'When putti told me, I dismissed it. I thought...putti had misunderstood.'

'He went missing in the forest', my father said hoarsely, barely hearing my mother. 'The forest officials found him after ten hours. He is lying on a slab in some morgue because the police and doctors are not releasing his body. They think he was murdered. Because his tongue is missing. No wild animal attacks like that.'

I recoiled in horror. Maybe if he had died in a car accident ... yeah that would've been a coincidence. Not this. No. This was directly connected to me, to Vrka ... I did not know how yet. Vrka was some kind of a subconscious projection of mine ... that much I understood. There were all kinds of brain shit people talked about—telekinesis, ESP and whatnot. What if my thoughts had been so powerful that somehow, I managed to personify them as Vrka? And, like a remote control that could explode a bomb from afar ... what if I've used this figment of my imagination to harm people? The more I thought about this idea, the more convinced I was of its veracity. After all, did I not have the most vivid out-of-body ... or near-death experience? What if my father was right? What if, in my anger, I harm my family too?

I don't remember much after that evening. Dr Swarna told me later on that I'd had some kind of a breakdown. I remained unconscious for two days. They were worried that I had slipped into a coma, but were perplexed since all my vital signs were steady. They hooked up an EEG monitor to my scalp to read my brain waves. The neurosurgeon said the readings showed delta waves—I was in deep sleep. 'It was your body's way of preserving you from the shock', Dr Swarna told me.

It was during that unconscious period that I saw Vrka for the last time. It was a very lucid dream. Or perhaps hallucination—a 3-D hallucination. Yes, Vrka was not just a dream; I could always feel his touch, hear his voice, breath and heartbeat. How could he be just a dream? Anyway when he came to me, he had the face of the wolf. Traces of blood still remained on his muzzle and he looked ferocious, yet regal. He was dressed in strange silken robes and sat on some kind of a throne. I had a sense of other beings; there was a strange kind of thrum in the air. I did not feel afraid though, but I did feel awe, as if I was in the presence of a great power. He lifted his head and howled. This was followed by celebratory howls of the other beings. Then, he looked at me (I was sitting up in my hospital bed, as strange dreams go) and even though he gave out a throaty growl, I understood what he said. 'He has been punished, my love.'

As I watched, the wolf-face disappeared and Vrka was back the way I knew him. He got up from his throne and walked towards me. I heard the whisper of his robes and took in the strange fragrance around him. He held out his hand, and I took it without hesitation. We were now on the stone mandap of Madhehalli. Everything was different about Madhehalli—there were no houses or streets. Only the temple stood by the dancing river. Far off, I saw a foaming, roaring waterfall, beyond which a creamy full moon rose.

'Who are you, Vrka?' I whispered.

'I am you, my dear. As you are me. You and I—we are as ancient as fire', Vrka said, brushing my lips with his.

'I don't understand ... '

Vrka turned to the moon, his profile aglow. 'I'm from far away', he said and turned to look at me. 'Here, let me show you. Look into my eyes.'

At first, his eyes were convex mirrors and I only saw my face. Then, I felt shapeless, weightless and poured into his orbs. I saw swirling dust clouds, exploding galaxies, spinning fireballs.

'Our race is as endless as time', I heard Vrka speak. 'Our Lord ... the Supreme Creator has visited this land numerous times to annihilate evil. You know about it. You have heard it. Sometimes The Creator came as a turtle. Or as a giant fish. Other times, He came as an emperor and a warrior. Our race has helped in His wars. Sometimes we appeared as a race of monkeys. Other times as bears. Another holy annihilation is coming soon. We have come to weed out the evil, lay the groundwork for His coming.'

'Take me with you', I whispered as a strange sense of urgency seized me.

'The moment is not ripe, my love', he said tracing my face with his fingertips. 'You have much work to do here. One day, you will hold my very essence in your hands. I'll come back to you on that day.'

I remember waking up disoriented with a momentary amnesia; I was unable to recollect why I was lying in a hospital bed. It all came back in a cloud burst.

Within a week of my discharge, my job with Helix Inc on DNA quantitation came through. I opted for a living quarters on their sprawling campus in the outskirts of the city. My parents protested, more out of habit I suppose. But it was different this time—I was not seeking permission; I was merely informing them.

My first home was a shoebox-tiny studio. To me, it was the grandest castle on earth. It was more than a collection of shelves, tiles, sofa and TV—it stood for freedom; rebirth. A place where I'd begin an internal journey, building my identity book by book, curtain by curtain.

Within a year of my joining, Helix Inc became the official partner for forensic research and development for the Indian Police. Soon, the cream of Helix staff, including me, was absorbed into the IPS to head state-specific forensic labs. My induction into the new Bengaluru-based forensic team took place on my 28th birthday. I was on government pay and perks, right down to an Ambassador and a driver, mind you.

That was probably the first time in my life I tasted unadulterated happiness—the happiness born out of shaping yourself into something incredible, despite severe discouragement from all around you.

I had finally reached that crucial fork in life—the junction where I could choose to discard the past and start a new journey. I wanted to rebuild my trust and ties with my family. I hoped my achievements would now be seen in a new light; they'd now be proud of me in the truest sense ... not just because of my fair complexion and facial structure—a genetic accident at best. I hoped they'd realise they were wrong about everything concerning me—from my decision to live on my own to working in an offbeat field. They had warned me that I couldn't cope; I did not know how to take care of myself—what would I do if I fell sick, or if I faced unwanted male attention, or if I had to change a light bulb? How would I manage? No! No! I couldn't do it.

It was a sweet, sweet moment of vindication when my Ambassador turned into our driveway. I was elated to see their curious faces. They were jubilant when I broke the news about my new job. But how could I forget their happiness always came with a condition?

'You must settle down now', Pramila aunty said. We were all seated for dinner. 'See we gave you enough time to get over those bad events. Now you have even achieved your dream. So you ... '

'I'm already settled, Pramila aunty', I smiled. But my birthday dinner had become quieter.

One of my uncles cleared his throat and said, 'Look, putti. Whatever happened, put it behind you. It is good you are enjoying your independence. But it is time you understood responsibility too. You are the eldest girl in the family. You must now think about your younger sisters. See Akshara, Isha and Arpita—they are already twenty-four. We have received very good proposals for them. What to do ... if everything had gone well, at least Akshara's marriage would have taken place two years ago only. By now, I would've been holding my grandchild. But we want to follow tradition—you are the Lakshmi of this house. We can't abandon you. We have to first finish our responsibility towards you.'

'Yes, yes. You just nod your head ... next year, we can get all four of you married in one go. How grand that will be!' Pramila aunty was probably already thinking of how many sarees she'd buy.

I had nothing to say, so I kept quiet; packing my disappointment and anger into a tight ball, wedging it into a small, dark corner of my bruised mind. The silence stretched. My uncle sighed, as if expelling his annoyance from his body.

'I hope you don't have to meet criminals in your job', my father eventually broke the silence.

'No. I work in a lab and process evidence.'

'What kind of evidence?'

'Fingerprints, isn't it?' one of my cousins asked.

'DNA matching and stuff', I said vaguely.

'Like those CSI episodes? Saliva, hair and all that?'

I smiled, nodded and changed the subject. But when I went to the kitchen to help do the dishes, I heard my father ask my cousin, 'What do you mean saliva? Does she have to touch someone's spit?'

'Not just spit', Pramila aunty interjected. 'Everything. Means all kinds of body things you know.' She lowered her voice and added, 'What do you think will be tested for rape and murder cases? I'm telling you, use your influence and see if she can get a job somewhere else. This is not a job a young girl should do. *Che!* Touching spit and blood and god knows what else.'

'I don't know what karma I have done to deserve this', my father replied.

They all became quiet when I emerged from the kitchen. I left early that evening. Well, I fled from the place.

I officially became an outcast the following year, during Akshara's wedding. My mother kept crying the whole time. 'It should have been you sitting in the wedding mandap', she said over and over again. My father refused to look at me—disgust largely writ on his face. My uncles and aunts refused to talk to me—I even missed Pramila aunty's irritating banter. My cousins were cautious when they spoke to me. I was completely isolated, ostracized. I left the wedding hall within an hour. My relationship with my family has been on a downward slide ever since.

More than the pain of losing my family, Vrka's complete disappearance from my consciousness gnawed at my innards all the time. I felt widowed. I wept for him. I visited Madhehalli alone, sat in the stone mandap for hours, staring at the pond, hoping somehow my stare would assemble atoms in his form. Even after all these years, I was unable to convince myself that Vrka was a part of my imagination. He was probably still in my brain, decomposed into electrical signals bouncing off neurons.

Six months ago, I'd woken up one morning feeling sick of my lonely life. I mean, physically sick. I wanted to come back to a home where I could make love to a man. Fight with him. Argue with him. Laugh with him. Burn the dinner for him. I was sick of all the hatred directed towards me. I am not a bad person, I yelled at the mirror. I deserved to be loved. Admired. Pampered. Not shunned like this. Like some whore. Bloody hell. If marriage was the answer to happiness, then so be it. I am sick of you Vrka, I yelled some more and threw things on the floor—books, coffee mugs and well, my laundry basket. I stood in the mess, breathing loudly for a couple of minutes. Then, I opened my laptop and looked up psychiatrists on NIMHANS website.

I randomly called one of them and booked an appointment for the next day. 'That's right, Vrka. I'm going to flush you out of my system. I'm going to get married to the first asshole I come across, have kids, have a healthy family life. I'm going to grin and fake-laugh through my family's conditional affection. But I'm NOT going to live like this ... like a discarded leper. DO YOU HEAR ME, YOU BASTARD?' I raged for some more time, the rage soon dissolving into tears. 'At least give me a sign, Vrka ... don't be so heartless', I sobbed. I got ready and left for work. 24 hours. That's Vrka's deadline, I thought. If I don't get any sign, I promised myself I'll never even utter his name.

There was a birthday treat that afternoon. Vinodini's birthday. She was my lab assistant. Fifteen of us went to a newly opened Indo-Chinese restaurant with one of those eat-all-you-want buffets. As usual, Varun, one of my colleagues from ballistics, became the butt of jokes—he was the epitome of gluttony when it came to buffets. Someone called him Bakasura. He shook his head and said, '*Che!* Don't make me a rakshasa. I am Vrkodara.'

'Vrka ... who?' one of the girls giggled.

I choked on my food, tears stinging as I gasped and coughed. Everyone laughed—they thought it was my comical reaction to Varun's rejection of Bakasura.

'You young people', Varun shook his head in mock-exasperation. 'You know only Game of Throne characters. At least you know Mahabharata, right? Bheema is also known as Vrkodara. The one with the stomach of a wolf. Vrka is Sanskrit for wolf.

I felt faint. I managed to extricate myself from the lunch party as quickly as possible and rushed home. 'You gave me a sign ... didn't you?' I whispered over and over again. I was at once ecstatic and afraid. What was happening around me ... to me? Questions gave rise to more questions. I desperately wanted to see Vrka. Maybe if I did some kind of a meditation, I could ... kind of ... manifest him? I called in sick, turned off my mobile phone, removed the SIM for good measure. Meditation was futile. My mind was buzzing around like a fly caught in a bottle.

I took on extra cases at work—that was the only way I could control my mind. Ever since that 'sign', I've been waiting ... waiting for something to happen. I could feel it, like static around my fingertips. Oh well. Who knows? Maybe I just have a tumour in my brain that makes me hallucinate. Maybe I was close to dying. I kind of felt glad.

So ... that is my story. Like I said, a strange life for a 32 year old. I don't know how this is going to end. Most probably suicide ... with this level of madness. Not a pleasant thought at 3 am on one's birthday—but it is what it is. I switched off the lights and sat in the darkness for a while.

I'd barely snuggled under the duvet when my phone rang. At this hour, even a pleasant flute ringtone sounds like a funeral tune. The commissioner was on line. 'I need you in the lab immediately', he said. 'Get a change of clothes; don't leave the lab till I explicitly ask you to.' The fear in his voice had me moving fast.

Even before the call ended, I saw headlights sweep across my living room. I was out of the door in ten minutes. They'd sent a *neeli bathi*. Something had happened. Something bigger than the usual shit-hits-ceiling. Whatever it was, I was glad in a perverse way. It meant I could skip the meet-your-potential-groom birthday dinner my family had planned for me.

The new forensic lab is in a quiet by-lane off Kasturba Road, Bengaluru. It has all the hallmarks of a government building—bougainvillea, rose shrubs and croutons hemming the compound wall; a soft lawn where a green water pipe perpetually lay across; a stone sculpture representing the river Cauvery holding a *bindige*, with water trickling out of her pot. The lobby and reception areas have smiling photos of assassinated prime ministers and political leaders, overseen by Mahatma Gandhi.

This was a new building and housed the ballistics and cyber crime divisions in the first two floors. The third floor was getting renovated to include behavioural units. My lab mainly dealt with physiological forensics—DNA and fingerprint analysis—and was nicknamed The Netherworld. It was two levels underground—India's first subterranean forensic lab. The first level housed the bomb squad.

For security reasons, there were no stairs to The Netherworld since we handled very sensitive evidence. The access was through a lift which could be activated only by a biometric card. In case of fire, our emergency exit was through an underground tunnel. No one knew where this tunnel ended.

I stepped out of the lift onto my floor. Despite working here for four years, I still flinched at the whiteness of the The Netherworld. I walked down the corridor to my lab, accompanied by my distorted image on the glossy white wall. The security camera, also white and hardly bigger than a golf ball, tracked me with a red, unblinking eye. I gave a flying kiss to the camera—that was for Rajeev Shetty manning the security controls—a hopeless flirt and a great friend.

'Bio Forensics' was printed unpretentiously above a bulletproof glass-panelled door. 'Dr Ratnaveni M.K.—Chief Forensic Analyst' was embossed on a metal panel next to the door. I wondered if my parents would finally feel a sense of pride if they saw my lab. This lab required the highest level of security clearance, and I was one of the only fifteen civilians in the country who had this access. Even the home minister could not enter my lab if I chose so. Needless to say, the ego rush was intense yet very momentary when I saw the commissioner waiting for me near the door. The door hissed open after my retina scan and I stepped aside for the commissioner to enter first.

I saw my assistant Tanya hunched over a large manual. She stood up when the commissioner cleared his throat. 'This will be a one-on-one meeting', he said curtly. Tanya looked at me.

'You can go home, Tanya. I'll call if I need anything.'

'I started work on the back-up sample. The tube is in the bath. It should be ready in thirty minutes for extraction.'

'Thanks, Tanya. I'll take it from here.'

We waited for Tanya to gather her things and leave. The minute she left, the commissioner sat heavily on one of the chairs. He handed me a thick file folder.

'What is this?'

'What do you know about this serial killer case?'

I looked at the commissioner with disbelief. 'Are you saying ... ?'

'Yes. We caught him two days ago. Well, I can't say caught. He walked into the High Grounds police station, blood all over his face. And surrendered. We sent his saliva swabs to your lab two days ago.'

'You should have received the results by now', I frowned. We had strict service levels in this lab.

'Yes, yes!' The commissioner waved his hands impatiently. 'That is not the problem. The DNA match report was sent to us a few hours ago. The problem is ... the sample we took from him seems contaminated somehow.'

'Is that why Tanya was working on the back-up sample?'

The commissioner shrugged. 'Or ... don't get me wrong ... maybe your assistant did not run the tests properly.'

'Impossible!'

'Or ... there has been a deliberate misinterpretation of the results.'

I crossed my arms and stared him down.

'Okay, okay! I'm sorry, that was nonsense. Look, you'll be given a fresh saliva swab. We are also giving you a strand of hair for good measure. I want you to personally run the tests. The media has no clue that he's been arrested. We are maintaining air silence on this one. Also, go through the case files. There are many details of the killings which have not been released to the media. You will be the prime forensic witness for this case. I want you to be thorough with every killing.'

I nodded.

'I will leave after the sample arrives.' The commissioner stood up and yawned. 'Is there a place where I can get a cup of coffee around here?'

'There's a coffee machine at the end of the corridor', I said, as I pulled on the forensic uniform over my day clothes. 'I'm afraid you can't bring it inside the lab though. I'll get on with prepping the work area.'

Half an hour later, my work area was ready but there was still no sign of the samples. I decided to read the case files. Why would India's most wanted serial killer surrender himself, I thought, as I opened the first file. Maybe he wanted to stop, trapped by his own insanity. Twitterati had christened him Jai the Ripper and the related hashtag had been trending for quite a while. Media reports claimed the killer hunted and attacked like a predator. He'd first go for the throat, severing the jugular and eventually ripping the internal food and wind pipes.

The killings were initially reported in the NCR corridor. In some cases, the victims belonged to a floating population—out-of-town labourers. I'm not even sure if the police continued to investigate their deaths—these were people with no identities, so to speak. It was only when similar deaths were reported in other metros, a special probe team was formed. Eventually, the recent murder in Bengaluru acted as a catalyst in the whole investigation. The victim was a boy from a very well-to-do family.

The killings had the same modus operandi; they were almost ritualistic in nature. The victims were all men—the youngest was 17, the oldest 56. Given that the victims were spread across India, police initially speculated a gang was behind the murders. It took a trainee journalist to link the victims—they were all sexual offenders. Some were on the police files—rapists out on bail. The victims in the hinterlands did not have any police records, but the local villagers alleged they were rapists. This news was sensational—a vigilante serial killer on the prowl. The country burst into debates—many in favour of not catching the killer; he seemed to be doing what the police had failed to do. No one knew what he looked like, but he'd become a renegade hero of sorts.

The commissioner was back after his coffee. 'They should be here any minute', he said, more to himself.

'You said some details of the killings were withheld from the media. What kind of details?'

'He did not go at their throats first. He ... look, I'm sorry you have to hear all this. Whatever was reported in the media is not true. At least, it's not the complete truth. For example, their throats were not ... hmm ... severed.' The commissioner pulled a chair and sat facing me. 'He first ripped their tongues out. According to the post-mortem, their brains were removed through their nostrils.'

The room began to spin around me.

I recollected that day in the hospital, me lying with my swollen lips and bruised mind; my father's hoarse voice, thick with fear, informing me that Surya's tongue was missing when they found his body. My family never spoke of Surya in front of me but I knew they were in touch with Surya's parents. I'd overheard a conversation between my father and Surya's father. The missing tongue detail had been a leak—information bought in exchange for a crate of imported whiskey from the constable who had taken Surya to the morgue. My father and uncles had tried many tricks to get more inside information, from offering cash to engineering seats in posh colleges. Nothing worked. Apparently, the investigation had become airtight, and my father had even been warned to stay away. Surya's killer was never found. The suspect, at least according to my father, was one of Surya's friends, the son of an industrialist. 'Only his family is capable of putting this kind of pressure', I had heard my father tell Surya's father. 'I bet they have bought out the entire investigating team.'

I never understood why my family was so interested in Surya's case, especially after what he'd done to me. As far as I was concerned, Surya was the black hole of my life.

'I don't even know how he managed to do it ... I mean how can you pull out the brain like that?' the commissioner looked bug-eyed.

'It's nothing new', I said, still lost in my thoughts. 'It's a very ancient practice. Egyptians had mastered it. You insert a hook through the nose and fracture the ethmoid bone ... it's a plate separating the nasal cavity and the brain. Once that hole is made, you can literally scoop out brain matter.'

'My God! I can't understand ... why not just castrate the bastards? Why go for the brain?'

I shivered. 'Maybe because the root of all goodness ... and all evil is up here', I replied tapping my temple. 'Every other body part just does the bidding of whatever is generated up here. You destroy that and the very generator of consciousness, thoughts, and actions perishes.'

'But why rip their tongues out?'

I looked at the commissioner. He seemed to be aging by the minute. I could not imagine the pressure on him for this case. 'To prevent them from screaming. In my opinion ... the victims were alive long enough to realise what operation was being performed on them.'

'My god! My god! But you know what? I am not saying this

as a policeman ... but as a human being. He delivered justice. The crimes committed by these men were of the most depraved nature. I won't even go into the details. Some of their victims were children. 6 years. 3 years. I can't tell you officially, Ratna. But I myself had a good mind to drag my feet on this case. I don't know why he surrendered.'

I was barely listening to the commissioner. I logged into a database to pull up Surya's post-mortem record. I did not know the case ID number, but I gave an approximate search criteria based on the date of death and name. I had his report in less than twenty seconds. Surya was missing his brain too.

'What is it?' the commissioner was alarmed by my expression. 'You are almost about to pass out. Shall I get you something? Water? Juice?'

'No', I trembled. What the hell was happening? Surya was killed by this serial killer? How did the killer know about my assault? Maybe Surya had other victims too.

The commissioner came around and peered into the computer screen. 'What is this? Is this related to the case?'

'Maybe', I said vaguely.

I pulled up the DNA test results of the sample that Tanya had worked on and enlarged the DNA sequence pattern. 'This is the DNA sequence of the sample you had sent across. This is directly from the perpetrator.'

'Yes ... the one that was contaminated.'

'Let me explain', I said, almost talking to myself. 'We have two sets of DNA sequences, right? The first one is swabbed off the victim's body. Maybe the perpetrator's hair or skin cells were found on the victim. So far you are with me?'

The commissioner nodded.

'Okay. So the second DNA sequence comes from the perpetrator himself. You had sent buccal swabs. Correct? Now, we say there is a match when both these DNA sequences are exactly the same. So when you say contamination, I'm assuming there is no match.'

The commissioner shrugged.

I frowned at the image. Yes, there was something wrong. I mean, I'd seen enough DNA sequences to know that I was seeing a gibberish sequence.

'According to Tanya's note, this is the DNA from the buccal

swab. This came right from the perpetrator—and yet, the sequence is rubbish. Which idiot took the swab?'

The commissioner did not reply.

I clicked on some menus and pulled another DNA sequence. 'This is the DNA sequence of the perpetrator that was swabbed off the victim's body. Hair and external skin tissues ... ', I trailed off. This sequence too looked weird.

I superimposed both the DNA sequences. There was a perfect match. 'What the hell?' I mumbled.

'What? What is it?'

'There is no contamination. See here ... see how the DNA bars of both samples align perfectly?'

'Then why did your assistant say the samples were contaminated?'

'Because this is not a normal human DNA.'

'Eh? You mean he had some disease or something?'

I did not reply. I clicked on some of the windows that Tanya had minimized. Clever girl, Tanya. On a hunch, she had fed the perpetrator's DNA sequence to a genome database. The database held the genome sequences of most known species on earth—it was designed to match a given DNA sequence against all genome patterns and identify the species. I opened the results window. It said 'Unknown Species. Click here for more details.' I clicked on the hyperlink. A photo of a wolf stared back at me. My heart started hammering like a piston. The system informed me there was a partial match for the genome of *canis lupus* and *homo sapiens*.

'What? What is it? Talk to me, Ratna. What is this lupus?'

'*Canis lupus* is the scientific name for wolf', I almost whispered. There was a strange buzzing inside me, as if some internal radio was being tuned.

'Wolf? Are you telling me an animal was involved in these attacks? Is that why your assistant asked if the latest victim was found in a forest area? He was actually found in his bedroom. It is animal DNA, isn't it?'

I felt faint. I wished the commissioner would go away. I did not realise tears were streaming down my cheeks.

'What is it? You better talk to me!' The Commissioner's voice was thick with fear.

'I don't have brain tumour. I did not hallucinate. He was always there with me.'

'Who? What are you talking about … ?'

I wiped my tears and stood up. Tanya had said she'd started on the back-up sample. I walked over to the warm bath equipment where she'd fitted the Eppendorf tube. I held up the tube. The lysis solution had broken down the cells in the sample. A cloudy precipitate floated at the surface—the DNA … his DNA. His essence.

'Vrka', I said. 'Take me to him.'

'I will come to you', a voice said inside my head. The buzzing inside me cleared. I felt I was now tuned to the right frequency.

The intercom crackled and the commissioner picked it up. I saw his face pinch into a knot. 'What do you mean he has escaped? There is no chance. It looks like a lot of insiders are involved. I want the names of everyone on the security roster. I want them suspended without pay pending investigation. I will come immediately', he banged the phone and stood still for a minute.

A muted wailing filled the air—that was the security alarm. An announcement sounded on the walled speakers. 'The alarm has been sounded as a precaution. All CCTVs are out. Request all to remain at workstations. Repeat. Request all to remain at workstations. Department leads to take immediate headcount. Repeat. Department leads to take immediate head … ' static filled the air before the speakers died out.

The lights went out almost immediately. The computer monitor threw a weak glow that hardly penetrated the darkness of the lab.

'Ratna?' the commissioner called out. 'I can't even see you.'

I did not reply. I was pulled into a fierce embrace, my ears once again pressed against his chest, those heartbeats making a familiar music.

What strange future awaits me? I don't know and it does not matter. All I know is I'm going to a place where time does not exist. A place where nothing can hurt me. A place of endless love. At last, I'll be going home.

# THE STORYTELLER

I stare at the cement bench covered in pigeon shit and spot the dim outline of the granite slab embedded in the backrest. Years ago, when the bench was new, the granite slab was a shiny black mirror inscribed with the words 'Dedicated to the courageous people of Thirukadal'. Four cyclones and many pigeons later, the words have disappeared. The place is so choked with weeds that the bench appears to rest on the thorny plants. Behind me, beyond a muddy track, the Bay of Bengal hisses and sighs in a treacherous language.

I look up at the sky, as if to decode the time. My watch says it is half past seven in the morning, but the sky, clotted with grey clouds, remains secretive. It could be evening as far as the heavens are concerned. A depressing form of rain is assured; the kind that only occurs in this eastern coast of South India—skies that sob continuously for forty-eight hours, increasing humidity, mosquitoes and the stench of choked drains, damp walls and wet clothes. I wonder if the sky had been just as morose on the morning of 26 December, 2004.

I tie a handkerchief around my face, covering my nose and mouth, and hack away at the weeds. Swarms of mosquitoes and flies rise in a static buzz and hover over my head like a satanic dark halo. It takes me an hour to clear a small area around the bench. The sky starts its weeping just as I scrub the bench with a coconut husk and Vim detergent powder.

After half an hour, the granite slab gleams into existence once again. I've got my memorial ritual paraphernalia in a Food World plastic bag. I bring out a strand of jasmine that I loop around the granite slab, its fragrance weak in the rain. I crouch under my umbrella that won't open fully and light a couple of incense sticks. I've forgotten to bring the incense holder, so I stick the smouldering incense into a banana that was to be my breakfast. I place it on the bench in front of the granite slab and hold the umbrella over it. I close my eyes in an attempt to pray. All I can think of is the angry allergic rash that's spreading on my legs and hands thanks to the weeds, and that the incense smells like a cheap aftershave.

I give up and sit on the bench, still holding the umbrella over the incense. The rain stings my skin like the rash. The hard, wet seat numbs my thighs instantly and a dull arthritic pain blooms in my knees and lower back. I squirm, shifting my weight from one butt cheek to the other. I wait, just as I've waited in vain for the last seven years, for the storyteller to show up. The incense is all ash now. I may as well eat the banana and tell you the story of how I met this mysterious man.

I'm an agarbatti salesman. I know it does not sound very ... what do you say ... prestigious. Boss, let me tell you one thing— your software-geeftware, finance-geenance, everything can do a Titanic. But not food and religion-based business. In fact, deeper the recession in the market, people pray more and more, and so agarbatti business soars. Anyway, I'm a successful agarbatti salesman. I'm just thirty-four years old and I already have a two-bedroom house with mosaic flooring in Mayladuthurai. The instalment for my Yamaha bike is done—the bike is fully mine. In two years, I can bet you your underwear that I will have a car. I started my career on the floor so to speak, as a fifteen-year-old rolling agarbattis. When I first became a salesman at twenty-two, I went around my area on a rented cycle. Then I got TVS-50. Second-hand. From that, straight to bike. Boss, tell me where you can have a career graph like this?

Eight years ago, in 2007, I was promoted as the zonal sales manager of Kumbakonam Aromatics Ltd. Actually, we were just Kumbakonam Agarbatti till the late nineties. Then we diversified. We do attar, room sprays, car sprays and all that—hence 'aromatics'. However, the bulk of business is from agarbatti only.

I still remember ... it was my boss, Uppliyappan saar, who called me on my mobile to give the good news of my promotion. 2007 Christmas evening, to be precise. I was near Velankanni, overseeing the bulk distribution of a Christmas-special agarbatti to retailers and hawkers. With more than a hundred thousand devotees visiting the Velankanni church, I had to ensure the retailers were well stocked. It had been my brainchild to make the Christmas-special agarbatti exclusive to this region. We had rolled out a trial run last quarter, and our quarterly profits had shot up by a neat nine percent. Of course, I deserved the promotion, but I did not expect a windfall that evening. Uppiliyappan saar had kept the best part for the last. Very mischievous man. He informed me casually that I was now eligible for the company loan to buy a Yamaha bike ... at minimal interest, mind you. Not just that, I was to receive an immediate cash bonus of twenty-five thousand rupees. I thanked saar over and over again and sat on the footpath, breathing heavily and laughing loudly.

Even though I'm a devotee of Ayyappan, I went to church that day. I had to convey my gratitude to Ayyappan, and if it was through Yesu , so be it.

I set off for my home after watching the sunset from Velankanni beach. Back then, I stayed in a rented house in Mayavaram near Mayladuthurai. For these long journeys, I almost always borrowed my brother-in-law's Kinetic Honda; my battered TVS-50 did not go beyond 45kmph. I think it was half past six when I started. With reasonable traffic, I could reach home by eight—just in time for dinner. But it was Christmas; I could not even turn into the state highway SH67. The unwritten laws of Indian traffic say that if a two-wheeler cannot pass through a traffic jam, then there is no hope at all. Instead of wasting time inhaling exhaust fumes of trucks and buses, I decided to take a detour through Karaikal.

I drove for about fifteen minutes, only to run into another pile-up on SH49. It was already seven fifteen by the time I was done with this circus. Fed up, I decided to explore a new route. 'New' means it was not a new road; it was simply an unused route. I believe it was a main road once, connecting Velankanni, Nagapattinam and Karaikal. The road had always been in a bad shape. So much so, even bus drivers had gone on strike saying only army tankers can go on that road. I think the government put some tar-geer and it was okay for a while. Then the tsunami happened and the road is now in the belly of Bay of Bengal. After that, no one dared to go on this route—not even the lovers who seek privacy.

For about ten kilometres, the ride on this unused route was okay, slow, but manageable considering the potholes—some were deep enough to strike oil. There was the sea to my right and a stretch of jungle trees to my left, so it was pleasant I must say. One of the IT companies from Chennai had planted the trees after the tsunami to help curtail erosion. I had watched this on Discovery Channel.

After ten kilometres, the road almost disappeared. It was sand everywhere. Now I was worried. It was twilight and driving on this sandy stretch was risky. What if the sand concealed some nasty pothole? Worse, what if my vehicle broke down? I was too bugged to turn around and go back to the choked highway. I stopped and thought for a minute. The trees and the waves took turns hissing and sighing and I got goosebumps. I decided to turn around and head back to the highway. Only, I did not.

I'd spotted footsteps on the sand. Several footsteps. It meant the road was navigable. I drove on, slowly, keeping my eyes peeled for the imprinters of those footsteps. A few minutes later, I heard muted music. It was an old Tamil movie song. Was it Sivaji Ganeshan's? I could not remember. Probably MGR.

As I turned a bend, I rejoiced. I had spotted a roadside hotel of sorts. It was really a shanty. The music came from a transistor radio placed on a plastic water drum. Empty plastic chairs were upturned on the sand. A boy squatted by the water drum, washing plates and glasses. A reasonably well-dressed man sat on one of the chairs, pulling in deep puffs from a cigarette and looking out at the sea. Two empty glasses lay at his feet.

As I approached the shanty, the man turned and stared at me. He was young—perhaps my age. He was dressed in a full-sleeved white shirt with thick pinstripes and black trousers. He was barefoot—a pair of scruffy black shoes lay next to his chair, plugged by balled-up socks. He gave me a small wave and I stopped.

'Escaping the jam on the highway?' he asked cheerfully.

I parked the Kinetic on the side stand and got down. 'Yes. You know this route?'

He took a puff and let out the smoke in a ring. We both watched as the ring dissipated. 'I always take this route', he said. 'It's bad for another two kilometres, but after that the road is quite good. You can reach Karaikal in no time.'

I pulled up a chair and sat down. I felt as if I'd driven a hundred kilometres. What a horrible end to the day, I cursed.

'Thambi', the man called out to the boy doing the dishes. 'Get a cold soda for brother here. One for me too.'

The boy, attired in a frayed t-shirt and lungi, immediately came forward with two bottles of Thums Up.

'Do you have anything to eat?' I asked.

The boy scratched his head. 'Saar, if you can wait for some time, I can make fish fry and gopi manjuran.'

My companion, the cigarette man, started to laugh. 'Thambi, it is gobi. Go. Bee.'

The boy giggled sheepishly. 'That's what I said, Raman saar. Go. Pee.'

I joined in the laughter. 'Okay. I don't eat fish. So just get some curd rice and your Go. Pee. Manjuran.'

'Wait, boy! Wait! I have company today. Let me also eat. Do one thing. Get venn pongal and your manjuran for saar. Make the fish fry for me. Go easy on the spice though. I can't keep running to the sea all the way to Karaikal.'

The boy left and my companion shook hands with me. 'I'm Raman Durai', he said.

'Murugan Sundaresan', I said. 'Do you work around here?'

'Yes, I work for an NGO. Trying to rehabilitate the village folks here.'

'There's a village around here?' I said, looking at the desolate landscape. The sky had turned aubergine; soon it would become pitch dark. I had second thoughts about my order. Maybe I ought to cancel it and carry on. I'd pay for it of course.

The boy lit a couple of Petromax lanterns and placed one near us. He hung one of them near the shanty and went inside. Soon, I heard chopping sounds, and the smell of onions sizzling in hot oil wafted, squeezing juices inside my stomach.

'We can leave together', Raman said. 'My vehicle is in the village from where the good road begins. The boys are repairing a puncture.'

I felt a bit relieved.

Raman hummed a tune along with the transistor radio. It was hypnotic in a way. The old song, the lanterns creaking in the wind, and me sitting with a stranger, watching the sea.

'So ... this entire stretch was hit by the tsunami, isn't it?' I said, trying to make conversation.

'Yes, yes', Raman looked at me. 'It was so terrible.'

'Were you there?'

'You know this place has a beautiful history. Have you ever come on this road before? Before the tsunami?'

I shook my head.

'Ah! Then I must tell you this story. It is a good way to pass time till thambi serves us our food.'

I smiled.

'See', he said, turning his chair towards me. 'Prior to December 26, 2004, 7:53 AM, this very spot had been a busy bus stop, popularly known as the Thirukadal stop. Oh, when I say bus stop, don't imagine a concrete structure. It was just a large, sandy clearing by the side of the road. At any time of the day, you'd see rusty and dented buses parked haphazardly, raising plumes of dust in the dry summers, or splattering slush during the monsoons. A dozen push-cart vendors sold pickled prawns, banana chips, lentil fritters, cut pineapples and jackfruits ... with a topping of buzzing flies. You can imagine the cacophony, yes? The metallic grunt of shifting gears, blaring horns, shrill voices of the vendors, Tamil songs blasted on scratchy cassette players in the buses and the occasional fist fights.'

'*Abba!*' I exclaimed. 'You are a very good storyteller, Mr Raman.'

Raman bowed his head as an acceptance of my compliment and continued his story. 'Most of the vendors were women—the wives of fishermen from the neighbouring village of Thirukadal. Some were old men from the same village who were no longer fit to go fishing in the Bay of Bengal.

'This bus route between Nagapattinam and Karaikal was very cheap. Lot of people worked in the Karaikal port from all these areas. So heavy traffic. The distance is just tonty ... tonty-five kilometres. But the buses would stop for every waving hand, stretching the forty-minute journey to one and a half hours. So this Thirukadal stop was a welcome and crucial break. As a bus passenger on this route, you would *have* to get down, despite the steaming stink of the prawns and the oily stench of fried condiments. You'd have to stretch and twist your spine and shake your arms and legs to get the circulation back, no?' Raman acted out the sequence with aplomb.

'I tell you why your circulation would be cut off. The bus would've taken a hundred and thirty passengers instead of the allowed limit of seventy. If you don't get a seat, then you'd be squashed between smelly armpits. If you were lucky enough to find a seat, the exposed springs would've twisted your coccyx.'

I laughed. Raman was definitely an entertainer. I had a feeling this was the beginning of an enduring friendship.

'There was a dense growth of parthenium weeds around the bus stop', Raman pointed all around. Of course now it was clear— only sand heaps everywhere. 'The weeds were well-watered and nourished by hundreds of men and women relieving themselves. The squeamish ones crossed the road and walked towards the beach', Raman pointed in the direction of the sea. 'If there was enough time for a bus passenger, he could find a quiet, secluded spot to complete No.2 business, with plenty of water at hand to wash up. Anyway, now you are seeing empty beach. But imagine a ramshackle group of huts. Some thirty of them. That was the Thirukadal village.' Raman stared at the waves for some time, probably imagining the village.

'One could smell this Thirukadal stop a kilometre away', he continued. 'That's when my NGO, Better Tomorrows, stepped in. I was designated as the liaison officer for the Thirukadal project. I was to work with the government to get a functional bus station at this spot. After intense lobbying, the government finally sanctioned funds for a modern bus station with tarred parking spaces, toilets, shopping centre and restaurant. Then, the elections took place and the government changed; the Thirukadal project went into cold storage. But by then, I was involved with many initiatives for the village—from literacy to health. I had formed a strong bond with the people—they had a streak of independence and ingenuity that I'd never come across anywhere. I especially became very close to Saktisundar, one of the finest fishermen I've ever known. We all called him Sakti. He was like the brother I never had. And, I fell in love with his wife.'

The static hiss of the waves filled the silence that stretched between us.

'People think history is all about warriors and kings; dynasties and empires', Raman resumed after a minute, almost talking to himself. 'But this here ... this bus stop, that desolate beach ... this is history too. History of the human spirit. You see, Thirukadal sprung into existence a decade after India won her independence. Karaikal and surrounding areas were not under the British rule but belonged to the French colony. Although India became independent in 1947, Karaikal joined the Indian Republic only in the 1950s, after an agreement between the British and the French. Anyway for many poor people, whose lifetimes rolled away in day-to-day survival, the politics of the land hardly mattered. Their existence revolved around waking up hungry and wondering if they'd taste food before nightfall, irrespective of being governed by the British, Dutch, Portuguese, French, Indians or indeed even aliens.

'In the searing summer of 1957, one such poor family set out to escape the drought in their own nameless village tonty kilometres away from Karaikal. Thirty-year-old Thangamani, his two younger brothers, his heavily pregnant wife Valli and a bony cow began their aimless walk in the general direction of the coast. They waved down passing bullock carts so that the woman could travel in relative comfort, while the men jogged alongside, dragging the cow. Finally they reached this spot which went on to become the Thirukadal stop. The person dropping them off had said, "Wait here, someone should be along soon because you are close to Karaikal. It's a big town with good jobs. And doctor for your woman."

'The family set up camp on the beach in order to have a quick lunch of millet gruel. It so happened that Valli went into labour almost immediately. The men carried her to a rocky outcropping on the beach where the boulders offered her some privacy. They watched helplessly as the woman writhed. But Valli came from a family of thirteen siblings, and as the youngest, she was no stranger to midwife duties for her ever-pregnant elder sisters. In between her screams, she shouted instructions to the men.

'On that blazing summer afternoon, as heat vapours radiated from the sand and sea, a healthy baby boy took his first gulp of salty sea breeze and let out a gusty cry.

'They decided to stay put on the beach till the mother recovered. The two younger brothers set off early next morning towards Karaikal. They walked for an hour before a bullock cart gave them a ride. Their journey was worth it. They promptly found jobs as coolies in the Karaikal fishing harbour. They bought provisions with their day's wages and returned triumphant.

'Sakti used to tell me this story whenever he was drunk', Raman gave a short laugh. 'Silly bastard. Two shots of country arrack and that's it. How it would loosen his tongue! "Do you know how Thirukadal was born?" he'd ask. In all the time I'd known Sakti, all his conversations started with, "Do you know this or that". Thangamani and Valli were his grandparents, and the hero of the story, the baby boy, was Sakti's father. Of course, depending on the strength of the arrack, the baby did extraordinary things the moment it was born—like crawling to the sea and riding the waves. But even without these additional spices, I found the story fascinating and always prodded Sakti to tell it.'

'What happened next?' I asked eagerly. This would be a great story to tell at home.

'So ... getting on with the story ... the three brothers quickly built a thatched hut on the beach. They decided to move to Karaikal in a couple of weeks, but it never happened. The baby seemed to love the sea and this place felt like home. Soon, other travellers began to stop by at Thangamani's hut for rest and shelter. Now Thangamani was a great storyteller. He told the travellers how divine intervention, in the form of the beckoning waves, had made him stop in this very spot. "I knew the baby will be born here," he'd say thumping his feet on the sandy earth. "The sea was boiling hot. This sand was like embers. But the minute the baby was born, cool air came from the sea. This sea air has medicinal qualities. See, my son has never taken ill."

'The travellers were so impressed with Thangamani's story that they too decided to set up camp in the same place. Karaikal was after all an expensive place. Here, they could build their own huts and not pay rent; their entire wages would be at their disposal. By the mid-sixties, a cluster of ten huts came up.

'"What is the name of this village?" a toothless old traveller had asked Thangamani.

'Thangamani thought for a minute while gazing at the sea as his son played nearby. "Thirukadal," he replied. Thiru was his son's name and *kadal* in Tamil meant sea.

'Thangamani died in 1975 followed by Valli soon after. Of the two younger brothers, one of them had returned to the village—the sea made him sick and it was said that the seabed of Bay of Bengal was completely covered by this boy's vomit. The other one had tried on a pair of sunshades at a village fair and decided he could become Tamil movie industry's next MGR. He ran away to Chennai and ended up as a dandy hotel waiter.

'But even as Thangamani's family dispersed, the village itself had grown. There were twenty-five hutments in 1975, with a population of sixty-five. Some of the fishermen erected more permanent structures with mud-plastered walls. As if to seal this sense of permanency, one of the villagers painted the name "Thirukadal" in Tamil on one of the boulders on the beach.

'Thiru was a young and formidable fisherman by then. He married Lakshmi, a vegetable vendor's daughter from Karaikal. Sakti was born in 1980. They called him Saktisundar because ... well ... Sakti told me he was superman who also looked like *manmathan*.

'Thirukadal came under Karaikal town administration sometime in 1985. In the previous census, the officials said there were too few children for the government to start a school here. The ten children of the village took a bus from the Thirukadal stop to Karaikal government school. But most would drop out before they hit their teens—the girls would stay back to help with the chores while the boys would join the men to learn the ropes of fishing. The village did not even warrant a medical centre, the officials decided. A medical camp was arranged once a month—government doctors from Karaikal would visit the village, shine torches into veiny eyes and peer into betel nut and beedi-stained mouths. If there were lady doctors then there would be unusually long queues ... the men would discover new pains everywhere.

'The '80s was also a decade of modernisation for Thirukadal. The road on which Thangamani had travelled was now a well-tarred state highway with street lights. Well, street lights meant electric poles and overhead wires—so it was quite simple for the villagers to draw power illegally from a nearby transformer. Electricity meant TV and radios. The villagers had to walk two kilometres to fetch drinking water from the Mallipoovu lake, but no one really thought it a bother. But if the TV went to the repair shop, then *aiyoo*! Thirukadal would mourn.

'Apparently, it was on one such Day of Mourning that Sakti met Andal. Sakti told me this story on a bus ride to Karaikal in 2002. No ... maybe 2004. Yes, I remember now. Thiru and Lakshmi had returned to their ancestral village in January 2004. Sakti and I were on our way back after visiting them. As usual, the bus made unscheduled stops and detours, and I was getting impatient. So Sakti elbowed me and said, "Do you know how I met Andal?"

'"Just tell," I laughed.

'"Very hot day in 2001, okay?" he began the story, enacting along the way. "I had come back after a ten-week fishing trip. All I wanted was a bottle of toddy and some good songs on TV. But TV wouldn't come on. Why? Because that Big Bum Bharani has dried wet petticoats on it. Now what to do? Magesh said some fair is going on near the Mallipoovu lake. At least some pretty town girls will be there no? So we went.

'"One side of the lake bank is on a higher ground. We go there to get better view. I spread a towel on a grassy patch and we sit eating roasted peanuts saying things like, 'See that one with two plaits and teeth like a coconut grater? What if she becomes your wife?' The toddy is working well. Magesh and I are laughing too much. Some people are doing boating. We laugh. Something happens and some of the boats capsize. We laugh. I am thinking it is just fun they are doing. Then I hear cries. It is real accident. Two children are missing and others are struggling to swim. Magesh and I rush to dive into the lake. That is when I see her. She is on the opposite bank. In a yellow saree with some flowers printed on it. She does not think twice okay—just removes her saree and dives into the lake in her petticoat and blouse. My God, I think. She swims like an eel. Two minutes later, she drags the children to our side of the bank. Everyone rush to pump the water out of the children.

'"She just stands there, wiping water off her face, breasts heaving, her taut navel quivering like a sail in the wind. Of course, every man was staring at her. This girl is a heroine, yes? So you have to treat her with respect, even if she is half naked and the wet clothes are more revealing. Then I go towards her. She sees me. And holds my stare. She knows I am struggling not to see

... you know. But her eyes are not lowered. This one does not feel shy. I think *dei* Sakti ... you have caught a shark today. I give her my towel. She just nods and takes it, covers her bosom and walks away. And I look and look and look ... and cannot find her. Her saree on the opposite bank is gone too.

'"After that evening, something happened inside me. I don't want TV. I don't want songs. I don't even want sea. I cry. I don't like food. I want to die. I want that girl. I become like the fish I catch ... can't breathe in air, right? Maybe it is karma, I think. Whatever suffering I give the fish, this girl has given me. Seventeen days I suffer like this. Seventeen. Hmm? Then she comes to Thirukadal. She is in a plain, green saree and black blouse. She has a jasmine strand in her plait. I want to act manly in front of her. You know, like, don't-care attitude. But my lips start to tremble when I see her.

'"I waited for you at the Karaikal port', she says, staring into my eyes. No introduction, nothing. Yes, I have caught a shark, I think. Look at the boldness of this one. 'Someone told me you live here.' I just nod, like a circus clown. I feel my feet have melted away. She is still staring at me. She asks, 'Is that your home?' pointing to my hut. I feel ashamed. How can I show this cave to a girl like her? I don't answer.

'"You know what she does? Brushes past me and goes and stands inside my hut. I follow her. By now, the villagers have gathered at our doorstep, sniggering bastards. She looks around. 'Build some shelves there', she says, pointing to a corner. 'And repair that thatch.'

"Why?' I finally find my voice.

"Because I said so. And because I'm going to live here.'

"But ... this is my hut.'

'She stares at me. 'Our hut.'

'"That's it brother. She did not go back. What do you think of this? Have you come across any woman like this? She is a shark and a tigress put together. If they make a movie, it will be super-duper hit."

'Soon after Sakti's fiery narration of his love story, I got to meet the leading lady. Usually, with the men away at sea for weeks, the women would gather around to make prawn pickles

and sundried poppadams. They packed these in big tin cans to sell
in the Karaikal market once a month. But they hardly made good
profits and wished they could go to the market more often. I was
called for a village meeting to discuss the possibility of getting a
loan from any local bank under women entrepreneurs' scheme.

'I was explaining the process to them when one woman stood
up. I knew it was Andal, although I had never met her before.
There was something about her, as Sakti had described, that was
markedly different. Perhaps it was the way she stood, or the way
she looked into your eyes, daring you to talk down to her. She
was petite, with a heart shaped face and eyes set like a deer's. Her
complexion was the colour of the sand on this beach, set off by the
cream nylon saree she had draped.

'"So what you are saying is we will get the loan after five
hundred years?" Andal demanded. There was some thigh-slapping
laughter in the audience. Without waiting for an answer, Andal
came and stood next to me, facing her people.

'"Between noon and three in the afternoon, some five buses
pass this road," she said. Her voice rode the waves. "Each bus has
hundred people—let us say. So five hundred people. What if we
are able to sell small packs of snacks every day? Even if we sell a
hundred grams packet at two rupees, and say only two hundred
of that five hundred buy it—we will still make four hundred per
day."

'The villagers were awestruck. Andal had proved worthy of
Thangamani's family. The next morning, they cleared the weeds by
the side of the road and stood displaying the condiments on push
carts. The first few buses did not stop, but eventually, they did begin
to park by the side of the road. That is how the Thirukadal bus stop
came into being', Raman snapped his fingers, as if revealing the
climax of a tense thriller. 'By then', he continued softly, 'I was in
love with Andal in the most desolate way.'

'What a super story, brother!' I said. 'It was like watching a
movie.'

'By 2004, the people of Thirukadal, with the help of my
NGO, were knocking on the doors of the district court to legalise
their land', Raman continued, barely hearing me. 'The state
government, however, wanted the community to relocate to the

suburbs of Karaikal. The rumour was that the villagers would be paid compensation to move.

'As the year drew to a close, the villagers looked to Sakti and Andal for guidance. "Let the goorment first show us alternate houses," Sakti said. "We are men of the sea, and we have to live near the sea. If goorment is able to give such housing, then we will take the compensation and move. Otherwise, they have to demolish Thirukadal over our dead bodies."

'I spoke to our NGO's lawyer and was told the judgment would be delivered after the Yesu festival. He had inside information that the people of Thirukadal would be given concrete housing, with internal plumbing. In addition, each family would be given a compensation of two hundred thousand rupees. When I announced this, the village erupted in a cheer. Andal rushed to me and clasped my hands. "Without your help this would not have happened," she said fiercely, her eyes glinting like wet charcoal. "This means our children can go to school safely. They will have a future. We can't depend on the sea all the time." I was barely listening to her. Her touch was searing me, constricting my breathing. As she walked away, I exhaled loudly. I caught Sakti looking at me. He knew. He turned away without a smile.

'The Yesu festival of 2004 fell on a Saturday. Considering it would be the last one they'd celebrate on this beach, the villagers planned a grand feast. I was invited as the chief guest. Even Thiru and Lakshmi came all the way from their village to join the festivities. Thirukadal was decked in lights and loudspeakers blared Tamil movie songs. The women gathered on the beach with large cauldrons to cook chicken sambhar and rice. In fact, there were only two Yesu followers in the village—Infant and David—and 25 December was the only time when either of them remembered Yesu. But each year, everyone pitched in for a celebration—for a community where sea was the god, religion really did not matter.

'At eight that evening, the village gathered around a roaring bonfire for the feast. David's incoherent prayer broke all previous records I was told, since it went on for fifty minutes. Just before the feast started, we realized the water drums were nearly empty. Some of the men were sent to fetch water from the Mallipoovu lake. They came back empty-handed, looking shaken. "The lake has disappeared," one of them said.

'We all ran towards the lake. Indeed, all we saw was a vast, clayey depression. There was just a muddy puddle on the lake bed. How could such a thing happen? Just that morning, the lake was very much there, a blue shimmering mirror, and the women had washed clothes on its banks and had drawn water for cooking.

'"It's a goorment conspiracy," Sakti thundered. "They want to throw us out before the court judgment. If they make the lake disappear, then we won't have water. So we will move. This will be considered voluntary, and they will not pay compensation. You whoring bastards," he turned to me and spat on the ground.

'The women started to cry. The men spoke of rioting and picketing a government office—any office for that matter. In an instant I'd become the outcast, the enemy, the government man.

'"No," Andal said calmly. "If you riot, they will arrest you. Tomorrow, let us call a water tanker to fill our drums. Then we will see what to do. When people with problems come on TV, the goorment acts fast. Remember that program on the slum in Karaikal? It came on TV and the goorment fellows came running to give electricity and water supply. We should also do the same. The TV office in Karaikal is next to the school where I studied. We will go there on Monday."

'Somewhat pacified, the villagers began to walk back. I lingered on—the unwelcome chief guest. Eventually, I too returned to the village. I wanted to catch Sakti alone and sort this out. But I lost my nerve; I sat away from everyone's sight, behind the boulders.

'After the women retired to their huts, the men continued to discuss the problem, at first quietly, then, fuelled by country arrack, they broke out into lengthy slurred speeches and patriotic songs. Eventually some of them passed out on the beach, while the rest returned to the warmth of their huts. I fell asleep on the rocks.

'I woke up just before eight the next morning, though it looked like the earth had skipped day-break. The sky looked diseased with oozing clouds. A hissing drizzle had started. I was perplexed by the silence. I could not hear the waves. Had the sea stopped breathing?

'I stood up, stretching my aching back. In all my life, I'd never seen such low tide; it was as if the sea had gone missing. It was so strange that I shivered. The seabed was exposed for nearly a kilometre and fish flopped and did their death leaps. Was the low tide so swift in receding that the fish couldn't keep up?

'"Sakti! Come and see this! The sea's gone!" I heard Andal shout. I climbed down the rocks and walked on the beach.

'"Good," I heard Sakti's sleepy reply, "we can walk all the way to Ceylon collecting fish."

'"Come here, Sakti. Sakti!" Andal was jumping and clapping her hands.

'Sakti did not respond. Andal snatched a bamboo basket and walked towards the gaping beach. I could almost hear her thoughts, "Sakti's face will be a sight when he sees my basket full of pompfret!"

'By then a few other women had stirred too. They looked at each other and laughed. Whoever had heard of a sea gone missing? Some of the men who had passed out on the beach continued to snore. I saw David kneeling in prayer, tears streaming down his cheeks as he attempted to sing a Tamil Yesu hymn between gasps and sobs. He saw me. "It is the way it happened to Moses."

'The wind picked up speed and howled, nearly ripping sarees and lungis. "I think we are in for a storm," Andal yelled over the wind. "Gather as many fish as you can—we will sell it in Karaikal market today."

'A couple of buses had stopped at the Thirukadal stop. The strange sight of the receded sea beckoned the passengers. They poured out of the buses and ran to the beach. Some of the men whooped as they ran on the exposed sea bed.

'I was still walking aimlessly on the beach, kicking the gasping fish out of my way. Something was not right, I thought. First the Mallipoovu lake, then this. I had to warn people to get out of the beach. By then, Andal's basket was full. I saw her straighten up. Our eyes met and she smiled. "Don't bother about Sakti. He did not mean anything bad," she shouted.

I walked over to her, feeling free and weightless. "Here, give me your basket. It must be heavy," I said, snatching it from her. "My! With this you can buy the Karaikal harbour ... what is it?" A look of anxiety had spread on her face. She was looking towards the sea. I followed her gaze ... and saw the strange, darkening horizon.

A black wall was rising where the sky met the sea. There was a strange whooshing sound in the air, something we'd never heard in the previous cyclone storms. It sounded like a giant jet engine that had come to life. Sakti would know what this sound meant.

'Andal turned around, the wind almost pushing her towards her hut. By then everyone on the beach had stopped gathering fish and stood staring at the sea. Finally someone broke the paralysis and yelled "Run!" The whooshing sound had turned into a rib-shattering roar', Raman shuddered at the memory.

I was too shocked to respond. So entrenched was I in the story that it took a good five minutes for me to realise that Raman had stopped speaking.

Eventually he broke the silence. 'For all my love for Andal', he said softly, 'for all my affection towards Sakti, the last thing I remember seeing on December 26 2004 is David kneeling on the beach.'

Raman stopped talking. He just sat there, staring at his palms. The silence became awkward and I checked my watch in the dull glow of the Petromax. I was shocked to see it was well past ten. Was I really sitting here for three hours? Whatever happened to our food? But I felt it would be inappropriate to talk about food after listening to such a tragic story.

'I ... I just don't know what to say', I said after the silence became unbearable. 'How many of you survived?'

'No one. Not a single one of us survived', Raman said without lifting his head.

I felt a great fear grip me; my body felt heavy as lead. To my horror, the sea had gone silent too. I could see the waves, but they were far, far away. An inky blackness surrounded us and a screaming wail arose. I tried to scream but was hit by such liquid force that I was sure all my bones were powdered. I felt the salty sea pour into my ears, nose and mouth, filling my lungs. I tried to swim, but it was as if I was tied to my chair, and I was swirling around in the deadliest maelstrom. Raman's body, along with other corpses, circled around me like sharks. I recognised Sakti and Andal. Half of Raman's face was gone. I knew my last moments were upon me. I tried to remember my family, but all I could think of was Andal running to fetch Sakti as the wall of sea rose like a serpent behind her. Andal came swimming towards me, 'Tell the world our story, stranger. Let them not forget us.' My lungs closed up completely and my body sank.

When I woke up, a roasting sun was overhead. I screamed out Raman's name as I came to. Only the sea responded with its characteristic liquid breath. I looked around. There was no shanty. No chairs. No lanterns. I was lying on the road, like some sozzled pisser. What about the soda I'd had? I distinctly remembered its lukewarm oiliness as I poured it down my throat. There were no bottles around me. Was this some kind of a prank? That's it! They must have added some drugs in the soda. My Kinetic! My wallet!

But nothing had been touched. My Kinetic was where I'd parked it. My wallet, with my debit card and two thousand rupees, was in my back pocket. I started the Kinetic and rode slowly. Raman, or whoever he was, had said there was a village after two kilometres. Of course, there was no village. But the road did get better, and before long, I was in Karaikal.

I walked into the first lodge I saw and booked a room for a couple of nights. My mobile phone had run out of charge, and the minute I plugged it in, the pings were incessant. 118 missed calls from home. I called home; my wife and mother were hysterical. I let them holler and wail for a couple of minutes. Then I told them to shut it or I'd smash the phone. When they piped down, I told them a friend's family had died in an accident. 'Entire family is wiped out. I am helping with the last rites. When the job is done, I'll call you women back', I said. 'Till then, don't call me because my brains are fried seeing the tragedy.'

I showered and had a large meal in the restaurant. I slept fitfully for the rest of the afternoon. Towards evening, I placed a call to Better Tomorrows NGO in Nagapattinam. They confirmed Raman Durai had been a 'stellar social worker'. Snatched away by the tsunami, along with the very village he had tried to save. I asked about the court decision on Thirukadal. 'It is such an irony', the voice at the other end told me. 'The court actually awarded five lakh rupees compensation for every family. The housing allotments were all near the sea, just as they had wished for.'

I went to a nearby temple that evening. 'Why me?' I asked as Vishnu stood resplendent in turmeric *alankara*. 'What am I supposed to do? You only show me the way.'

I thought a lot about Thirukadal, Raman, Sakti and Andal that night. By morning, I had a plan. As a sales person, I had a good network in the newspapers and magazine circuit. I called one of my friends who wrote for a popular magazine and asked him if he would do a story on a lost village. I met him for lunch and narrated the story. I told him vaguely that I had heard bits and pieces here and there. But he could corroborate with Raman's NGO and court verdicts.

I then went to a local builder, who was overseeing the construction of a multi-storeyed mall. 'If I want to get a cement bench made, whom should I ask?'

The man gave directions to a workshop. 'I don't know if they make benches—but they make cement dustbins.'

The workshop charged me eight thousand rupees to make the bench. Additional two thousand to fit the granite. Another three thousand for transport and installation. I flinched at the cost—the last time I'd spent this kind of money was to invest in gold for my twin girls. It's never too early to start saving, yes? But I also believe that every single paisa, every single morsel of food that comes your way is predestined. I guess I have some karmic connection with Thirukadal—their names were written on my promotion bonus.

'Okay, keep it ready', I told the proprietor of the workshop, handing over one thousand rupees advance. 'I will let you know the date of installation. Remember, the inauguration will be done by a very high minister. So better do a great job.'

'Don't worry. It will be fit for Tirumalai Nayaka himself', the owner flicked the towel on his shoulder to demonstrate his spirit.

After ten days, my journalist friend called. They had decided to run my story as the centre spread of their magazine. I told him about the bench. 'Will it be possible to have the judge who delivered the Thirukadal verdict to inaugurate it?'

'I will see what can be done.'

It all fell into place. On Sankranti of 2008, the bench was installed. The priest from a nearby temple performed a small ceremony. The judge spoke a few words and smeared vermilion on the granite slab embedded in the bench. We observed a minute's silence and dispersed.

From then on, every year on 26 December morning, I travel to this place to do my own memorial service. Every year, I hope to meet my storyteller again. I want to see if he's happy with what I've done. It is strange—the way I yearn to meet him, but also feel relieved that I did not meet him. How can one feel so much affection and fear at the same time? Perhaps if I could muster enough courage to come here on Christmas night ... that's when I'd first met him ... I might get to see him again. But I don't have the balls to come here after sunset. This year especially, I wanted to come in the night. I even drove half the way. But I thought about my little girls. What if something happened to me? I turned around and went home, dejected. This would be my last visit ... for the time being. I was being transferred up north to head the exports division.

The rain has stopped. The tears have started. I touch the granite slab one last time and walk away. I've parked my bike a few yards away.

It is only when I start the bike that I notice the footsteps on the sand. They appear one by one ... then many ... all surrounding my bike.

'Raman', I whisper. 'Sakti! Andal!' I call out. The footsteps spell out *nandri* in Tamil script—thank you. I pick up a fistful of the sand and pack it in my Foodworld bag. 'When I die, I want this sand to be on my body', I say aloud, my throat closing up in unbearable grief.

'Go in peace my unknown friends. Go in peace.'

The footsteps fade away.

# REMINISCENCE

Six thirty on a Tuesday morning and I'm still in bed, my mind wandering over this and that. What luxury, I think. I can hear Radha in the kitchen, grating coconuts. At seven she will peep in to see if I'm awake. Only then she will switch on the mixer to grind the chutney. You see, there'll be dosa for breakfast. Tomorrow, Radha will steam idlis with today's leftover dosa batter. This is the pleasure of retired life—the predictable routine.

On some days, I lie in bed almost till eight. Radha would call out and laugh. 'Are you compensating for rushing out at five in the morning for four decades?' she'd say. These are the mornings when Radha cooks vegetable upma for breakfast. Upma is like concrete ... *abba*! So heavy on the stomach that we usually skip lunch and catch a noon show at Tribhuvan theatre.

I hear the clang of the big steel stockpots. The mixer is on a shelf above the sink where Radha keeps these stockpots. Actually, stockpot is a fancy word I learned from my son. It is steel bucket only. There was a time when we'd have a lot of guests over for Dussehra or Diwali. On such days, rasam, *kootu* and sambhar would be cooked in these buckets, enough to serve twenty–thirty people. Those days are gone. Nowadays, it is a big thing if we get one or two visitors a year. Everyone is busy with their own lives. Besides, it has become a fashion to gather in hotels-geetels for lunch party. One way it is good only, otherwise the maid will ask extra hundred rupees to wash such big-big vessels.

But we have stopped attending even these hotel functions. First of all, getting an autorickshaw to ferry us to a place of our choice is difficult. Once I told the auto fellow, 'Tell me where you want to go, I will simply go with you. Let us forget my destination. Here I am ready, wearing nice shirt and pant. Let us go.' He felt ashamed of himself and finally agreed to take us.

Also, hotel food has another problem. See they put so much

soda-geeda in the food that I feel bloated for many days. Explosions are heard in my house and Radha keeps laughing and laughing. On such days, Radha only does all the shopping. 'What if you are in the market and let loose?' she had asked once, tears streaming down her cheeks—so much laugh comes for her. 'They will think some terrorist attack has happened.' So I avoid hotel food. I don't want Radha to roam around in the market with chain-snatchers on the prowl.

Anyway I keep telling Radha to give away the big vessels; we'll get a good exchange offer in Total Mall or Big Bazaar. Maybe we can get a carpet worth a thousand rupees for the living room. But Radha is adamant about keeping them. She bought those vessels by participating in some chit fund scheme with Pramod Steel Mart. She collected them over a period of ten years. She says the vessels remind her of a time when we always fell short of cash by the month end, yet, there was always food for anyone visiting home. Now, by Vishnu's grace, there is no shortage of money, but acute shortage of people who'll visit us.

I can hear Radha setting up the mixer. The mixer is very old—maybe thirty years. No, thirty-five years actually. I bought it with my first Diwali bonus in 1980, when we were residing in that rented house in Girinagar. The mixer is a local brand—Nisha. Those days, Philips-gillips and many such foreign-sounding brands were very expensive.

There was much excitement in the house when the mixer was unpacked. My Amma, who is now no more (may Vishnu bless her soul), smeared the mixer's power button with turmeric and vermilion as an auspicious gesture and prayed to Lord Ganesha to bless the mixer. The mixer was surely a sign of modernity and prosperity. It meant I was 'getting there'—another expression I have learnt from my MNC son.

After much discussion, it was decided that it's a good omen to inaugurate the appliance at an auspicious time by grinding something equally auspicious. Although Deepu, who was a ten-year-old then, suggested we could grind Amma only since she was the family elder and she'd always chant 'Krishna, Krishna' and hence she was most auspicious, we decided to grind grated coconut instead. We could use it to make *kheer*. After all, coconut is the most auspicious fruit, and *kheer* is most, most auspicious sweet.

Amma said we could do this at six thirty in the evening after lighting the lamps in the puja alcove. 'It is a time when Lord Narasimha will sit at the doorstep protecting us from evil eyes', she noted with conviction. So that day, the lion-man avatar of Lord Vishnu, who was presumably seated at our doorstep, was treated to the screech of the mixer grinder.

We lived in a working class neighbourhood, and our *vatara* consisted of ten houses enclosed in a single compound. Now the arrival of the mixer had to be celebrated—just the way when Shyam Sundar, our adjacent neighbour, had bought a ceiling fan. *Abba!* What an occasion that was! Four of us men helped Sundar hook up the fan. Then all the ten families of the *vatara* had gathered in his cramped living room, looking up at the rotating blades, marvelling at the cool breeze. Mrs Sundar distributed sweets—gulab jamun I think—after all, they were the first to own a ceiling fan in the *vatara*.

Shyam Sundar was a man about town, knew many things about many places. 'This is Usha brand ceiling fan', he said pointing to the fan. 'Best to buy Indian brands. My cousin Rohit ... that bald guy who does *bijness* ... bought a ceiling fan from Singapore. It has gold-plated designs on the blades, looks very beautiful. But it stopped working within three months. What is the use? He has put the blades in the showcase. This Usha is plain and white, but see the breeze. Wait, let me turn up the speed', he turned the speed to a maximum and we all gasped.

'Turn it off, Sundar, otherwise I won't go out of your house. It is so very, very nice and cool', I said.

'*Arre* what is there? This is your house only. You know, Raghavan, if I had fifty rupees more, I would have bought the model with four blades. This is basic model with three blades.'

And so we had all discussed and cheered and laughed—their happiness was our happiness.

Like that ceiling fan occasion, now also all the neighbours came to our home to partake the *kheer* and cheer the mixer. They praised the smoothness of the *kheer*. Savitri who lived above our house, and who was a bit fashion-conscious (just to come to our house she had put Vicco Turmeric and Ponds powder, according to Amma's hawk-eyed observation) said, 'Radha, this is really very good, like the nectar of life only.'

'You are too much, Savitri', Radha had blushed. 'But yes. See when we grind by hand with that grinding stone, so many coconut lumps remain in the *kheer* no?'

'Yes, yes. See now—this is smooth as satin. I will shamelessly have second helping, Radha. Your mister has made very good choice.'

'*Aiyoo*. Have all the *kheer*, what is there? I will make some more right away.'

Shyam Sundar gave his seal of approval on all the three steel mixer jars. 'You bought a very intelligent thing, Raghavan. See my cousin, Rohit ... that bald guy who does bijness ... I told you about him no? He bought a Korean-make mixer with colour-colour plastic jars. His four-year-old son is a bit naughty-naughty; in two days, he broke all the jars. What to do? Korean company has no spare-geer in Bangalore no? Full waste only.'

What can I say—for as long as we lived in the *vatara*, the mixer was used by all the families to make their masalas, chutneys and dosa batters.

Even so, thirty-five years is a long time for a mixer. Now whenever it is switched on, it wails and screeches, jarring bones and teeth. So Radha waits till I wake up before switching it on.

I have lost count of how many times this mixer has been repaired. Something will happen—the motor won't run, or the blades will go blunt. At least once in three-four months, I must be ready for this repair trip. It is like a pilgrimage—I have to take three buses and go to Chikpete, and then walk for a kilometre from the bus stop. There is one particular Marwari shop—a small one—only they do the repair. No one else in Bangalore is ready to even touch this mixer. The repair usually takes half a day. What to do—I will sit in the shop only, just reading the newspaper. If the big Seth is there, we chat a bit about politics. He complains about taxes. They give me tea and some nice-nice snacks like *khara sev*. They call me Mixie Uncle. It is funny; I have been going to this place for more than ten years, yet we don't know each other's names. Once the repair is done, one of the boys will drop me to the bus stop on his moped.

On several occasions, I wanted to give the mixer away in an exchange offer. But Radha would have none of it. Sentimental fool she is, Radha. Says the mixer is invaluable because I bought it with my first Diwali bonus.

'See this time we can buy Philips only', I tried to persuade her. 'See here', I showed her the brochure. 'It is very quiet. You don't have to wait till I wake up to run the mixer.'

'You are retired, do you remember?' Radha had retorted. 'Nine thousand rupees for a mixer. Why, is the Philips blade made of gold? If your hands are itching to spend money, just give it to me. I will put it in that post office insurance scheme.'

'But this Philips mixer is very intelligent. See it can chop all your vegetables also. See here, this photo. See how finely it has chopped the onions and cabbage?'

'No need. I still have two hands.'

I hear Radha pour water in the coffee strainer, and in an instant, the whiff of filter coffee fills the house. I think I'll start the day, but it is still 6:45 am. I can lie down for some more time; what is the hurry-burry anyway?

I watch the seconds hand move on the Ajanta wall clock above the window with its characteristic loud tick. I feel as if I'm floating and I can see the reflection of my face on the glass dial of the clock. Oh nonsense, I must be falling asleep again.

The clock is younger than the mixer. Only ten years old. It was a gift from Radha's brother. I can't remember if it was for our twenty-fifth wedding anniversary or for the housewarming ceremony. But I do remember putting it up.

I'm not very good at such jobs—all this nailing-geeling repair-gipair things. Radha had said we could wait for Deepu to do it, but I would hear none of it. 'We must not depend so much on Deepu', I told Radha. 'As it is, he is able to visit us only once a month. Let us not give him work when he comes home. Anyway what work I have? I will do it slowly, don't worry.'

'*Aiyoo*. I am not worried about you. I am worried about the wall', Radha had laughed.

I brought out the foldable aluminium chair. 'Hold the chair firmly', I instructed Radha as I stood on it gingerly and marked the spots where the nails had to go. As I started hammering the nails, Radha must've muttered a million times, 'Be careful, be careful ... watch your thumb, why are you doing this way? Why not that way?' *Abba!*

'Be quiet for a second!' I had yelled as I swung the hammer. 'This wall is made of iron I think, see. Nail only is bending.'

'*Aiyoo*. Forget the nail. See that plaster has fallen off. The wall has an ugly patch now.'

After four hours, I managed to fix the clock on the wall crookedly. It remained that way forever. Deepu had offered to set it right but Radha said no. 'Your Appa's first handyman job, Deepu', she had laughed as usual.

I think I put up the clock a couple of weeks after we moved into this house. Yes, now I remember, the clock was a gift for *grihapravesha* only. When we bought this house, the entire neighbourhood was empty. From the window below the clock, we could see miles of wild grass. Now this area has become a central place. Three or four people sold their sites to the same builder and the builder erected an apartment. Now I can only see a concrete wall through the window.

But what to do? We cannot change houses like clothes. Now the window has become a hanging place for a calendar. And Radha has put chiffon curtains. Actually in a previous avatar, the curtains were sarees. It so happened, while travelling in a bus, someone stepped on Radha's saree and it tore. So Radha did some embroidery-gimbroidery and converted the saree into curtain.

I was angry. 'You think I can't afford new curtains?' I had scolded her.

'You can afford many curtains. But this saree was gifted by Deepu. He bought it with his first pay, remember? How can I throw it away? You had bought that bangle set to match the saree? So many good memories no?'

Lined on the window sill are all kinds of tonics and multivitamin tablets that Radha insists I take. 'We are vegetarians. From where will we get proteins and iron? You hate spinach, radish and all the good things. All the time potato, potato, potato', she'd grumble as she fussed around me.

When we moved into this house, Radha refused to buy extra furniture like dressing table. 'The wardrobe has a full-length mirror. I don't need a dressing table to store one bottle of hair oil and one talcum powder.' There is no winning an argument with Radha.

But Radha's herbal hair oil (made of gooseberries and hibiscus flowers) was the same colour as Benadryl tonic. With my failing eyesight, I was sure I would either apply Benadryl on my head or drink the herbal hair oil. So to avoid the situation, we finally bought a dressing table.

'See now you can sit comfortably and comb your hair and apply your cream-geem', I told Radha. But Radha had other plans. The stool that came along with the dressing table became a stand for the steel water filter in the kitchen. All the receipts, bills, bank statements that found their way to the top of the fridge found a new home in the dressing table drawers. As a mark of respect for my sentiment, Radha placed her hair oil on the dressing table. Her combs and hair clips still sat on the window sill.

In fact, every object in this house—from a spoon to that Godrej wardrobe—has Radha's touch. Maybe it is too late, but I often think about the purpose of my life. In what way did my existence affect this world? I mean I did not cure diseases; did not invent things; did not go to the moon and mars. I feel a restless turmoil whenever I question like this. I cannot read Bhagwad Gita and Upanishads to find answers. I have tried to read, but I don't understand when they say 'ether' and 'otherness' and 'cosmic' and all that.

That is when my eyes wander over all these things—the mixer, the curtain, the dressing table, the clock—and I feel peaceful. To have loved Radha, and to have been loved by her—yes, that has been the purpose of my life. It is enough. It is enough. My eyes sting.

There! That floating sensation again. Must be low BP or low sugar or something. It will become okay once I have coffee. Sure enough, I hear Radha's footsteps. She is coming in to see if I'm up. I sit up, feeling as if I'm levitating.

Radha comes in and sits on the bed. I call her name, but she does not turn around. I see her shoulders are shaking, followed by those sobs that pierce my very core. Panic froths inside me. I want to pull her to me, but I have no strength in my arms. I can't feel my body. Sleep paralysis. I am sure it is iron deficiency. Of late this is happening—it is terrifying—this being awake, yet not being able to move.

Radha wipes her face with her saree. She gets up, walks around and smoothens my side of the bed. She picks up my photo from the bedside table. It is in a silver frame, with a sandalwood garland around it. She wipes the glass and places it back. She whispers my name over and over again, the empty room echoing her voice.

# HAPPINESS CLINIC

I lay awake, staring at the digital clock on the stool next to the bed; the red, pulsing seconds well-timed with my heartbeats. It was two-thirty in the morning. I hoped that counting the seconds would lull me back to sleep; if anything, I was more awake and alert. The bed creaked as I turned to lie on my back. The fan overhead made a metallic click with every rotation. Next to me, Sharada snored gently, oblivious to clicks and creaks. What if the fan were to fall on us? Why do I get such ridiculous thoughts in the middle of the night?

Sharada's snores had stopped. The room was quiet, except for the struggle of the fan. Had Sharada stopped breathing? I turned on my side to face her, the bed creaking in protest. I could see the gentle rise and fall of her chest in the dim glow of the electric mosquito repellent. I watched her for some time; she always slept on her back, a hand across her forehead, mouth open. Her snores started again.

Somewhere out on the street, a dog barked in frenzy. I knew the raspy bark—it was the three-legged dog down the road. The bark was picked up by other dog packs in the area, and the orchestra continued for about five minutes. The silence after this cacophony was deep, and I finally drifted off.

I jerked awake when the shrill blast of a whistle went off outside our window, followed by the slap of a lathi against the pavement. I sat up cursing, my heartbeat pulsing faster than the blinks of the digital clock. It was nearing four. Another blast of the whistle. Of course! It was the last week of the month. The gurkha would present himself in a couple of days demanding seventy-five rupees for keeping the area safe. No one knew who he was and who appointed him. I don't even know if the man who came to collect the money was in fact the gurkha whistling his head off outside my window.

I had argued on this point when he had come to collect the money last month. He is a fat fellow with a Veerappan moustache. He always comes in an old khaki uniform and a muffler tied around his head like a turban. 'Do you even know who gurkhas are? How brave they are?' I had raised my voice. It was not about the money—I guess I was just irritated to see him early in the morning, even before I'd had my coffee. 'You just blow your whistle now and then and want seventy-five rupees, is it? How do I know it is you only?'

'What, saar? I only have been coming for last two years. Ask *ammouru*, saar.'

'Who has appointed you? Who has given you permission to create noise in the night?'

'Saar, I don't have time to argue early in the morning. You are retired and have full day for this *jasoosi bijness*. If you want to see who it is, you come out when you hear the whistle. Just because you sleep well and don't hear the whistle, you are saying bad-bad things about me. You can keep your money in your pickle jar.' He turned around and left even before I could work up a sarcastic reply.

'Why do you want to pick up unnecessary fights? What if he brings a gang to threaten us?' Sharada had scolded me.

'Gang? What, you think this is movie-geevie? Let him come, I will break his legs and dangle it around his neck.'

Of course, deep down I felt afraid. One keeps hearing of murders of senior citizens in Bengaluru. But I felt ashamed too—I had noticed that fellow was wearing such worn out shoes, there was a gaping hole through which his toe poked out. He wore no socks. I could have been kinder.

Anyway, from then on, the gurkha retaliated harmlessly by standing specifically near my window and whistling like a steam engine. I guess he took out his anger on the pavement stones also. I wondered about the three-legged dog and its gang—not even a whimper when this gurkha roamed around.

Sleep was now a long way off. My nerves were still jangling from that infernal whistle. I went back to staring at the red digits on the clock. I wished we could sell this house and move to an apartment. There certainly won't be problems like these in apartments—all these dogs and whistles. But we have been on this street for more than thirty years. This house came as a housing board allotment, with the usual hallmarks—red-oxide floors, small windows, black Cuddapah limestones for the kitchen floor and jelly stones in bathroom. We made alterations down the years—changed the flooring to mosaic, increased the size of the bathroom to fit in a washing machine and things like that. But we can't change the basic structure, no? There is hardly three-feet distance between the house and the compound wall. So if you open the main door, you tumble out to the street. No security at all. Even a person with one leg and one hand can jump over the compound wall. So every time the dogs bark, I stay alert—what if some dacoits are climbing over the compound wall?

If I tell Sharada about this, she says let the thieves come. If they see the state of this house, they will only give us money.

The time was already 4:29:10. In thirty seconds, the temple down the street will start waking up gods and devotees alike, asking one and all to surrender to Lord Ayappa. There! That was the initial static in the loudspeaker. Ah! Now the frenzied chants have started. After an hour, one would get to hear S. P. Balasubramanium's devotional songs. This cassette is damaged, I suppose. In the third bhajan, SPB wept while singing some words backwards. There'd be some silence only by 7 a.m. But by then, Sharada's day will be in full swing. So what if Ayyappa has woken up on the street, inside our house Lord Narasimha should also wake up no? So Sharada plays her *suprabhata* and sahasranama and whatnot.

Maybe it was this lack of sleep that had made me irritable. This had become my favourite pastime—trying to understand why I have changed like this. From a gentle, amicable personality to someone who puts everyone on the edge. My family—Sharada, my son Sridhar, my daughter-in-law Rhea—has a theory that I have problems adjusting to my retirement. I get angry thinking about it; how simplistically they have written off this anguish I feel. I feel I have no grip on my life; I feel like a stranger in an unknown town; I search and search for an elusive happiness. But whenever I've tried to explain, they would all put it down to retirement—as if retirement is a disease.

S. P. Balasubramanium's weeping had started. It was nearing five thirty. Sharada would be up any minute now; I could make out the change in her breath. But today, even I had to get up early. We had to attend a marriage—my cousin's daughter. I don't like my cousin all that much, and the last time I saw his daughter was maybe fifteen years ago. But Sharada was quite close to them. It is strange actually; it was only after retirement that I noticed how popular Sharada is in my family circle. She knew all species of distant relatives on my side while I barely knew one uncle from the other.

Lord Ayyappa had woken up; there was a lull in the loudspeaker. Now, in our house, M. S. Subbalakshmi had started waking up Vishnu. I couldn't take it anymore. I flung the blanket aside and stomped to the bathroom. 'May as well get ready and sit like a doll', I cursed. Five minutes into the day and I was already angry; I felt a vast emptiness spread inside me.

The marriage *muhurta* was at 11:20 a.m. The wedding hall was in Gandhibazar, a stone's throw from our house in Jayanagar. Sharada wanted to go early to help in the preparations. 'I will leave at seven thirty ... you can come by ten or so ... no need for you also to hurry-burry', she smiled at me, adjusting the pleats of the kanchivaram, a safety pin in her mouth.

'Have you lost your head?' I said, more loudly than I intended to. I immediately softened, but the tone had done its job—the smile withered on her face. 'You know I will not send you alone in an autorickshaw.'

'Who will carry away a fifty-five year old woman?'

'Anyway, why should you go so early? Have they ever come to our house to find out how we are doing? Forget coming, have they even telephoned? Why ... only three months ago you were down with fever for a week. Did any of those fellows come to even give you a small cup of coffee? Why are you ... '

'Can't I go to a function peacefully?' Sharada's eyes were glistening. 'The last time I met all our relatives was two years ago. I want to go and just enjoy the day. How many days do I even step out of the house?'

'Okay, there is no need to cry for everything I say. I am saying for your good only. I will not speak anything from now on. I have become a big villain for everyone.'

Our ride in the autorickshaw was quiet—after forty years of marriage, it seemed like Sharada and I lived in different worlds; rather, I had banished her from mine.

Two years ago, I had retired from a long career as an accountant in a private firm that manufactured car auto parts. The first year of retirement was a breeze. Almost everyone had predicted that I would be bored within a week and would seek out employment again. Forty-five years of working for the same firm, forty-five years of the same routine, and forty-five years of the same faces ... what made people even think that I would get back into a similar job again? Perhaps it was my character—that of a sedate, non-controversial, non-confrontational, mild-mannered, mild-tempered, hard-working gentleman. Retirement was like pregnancy—there were advices from all quarters. Suddenly people were worried as to how I would 'spend time'. Why—I wanted to spend time with Sharada ... every minute of the day, as simple as that. I wanted to take her around, maybe an all-India tour for a start.

Well, the only trip we managed was this temple tour—Chidambaram, Palani, Rameshwaram and so on. I hated it. Just hated it. I have nothing against temples. When I broached the idea of a trip to Sharada, I had something completely different in mind. I wanted to take her to some exotic locales, stay in a good resort ... you know? But Sharada had innocently told this to other relatives and before long, fifteen people had jumped in and had decided on the plan and the itinerary. I had agreed amicably, as I had done in all confrontational situations throughout my adult life.

I guess that trip was the first turning point of my social deterioration. The only thing I remember from that stupid trip is standing. Standing, standing, standing. In queues. Either for the puja or for the prasadam. I was so distraught that I've never stepped into a temple again. From then on, life went downhill. All those things that I had planned to do ... well, everything evaporated. I became withdrawn; people irritated me and I reciprocated the sentiment.

Sharada thought that I was finding it difficult to adjust to the idea of retirement. She confided in my son and daughter-in-law. They wrung their hands helplessly. What had happened to the mild-mannered Seshadri they all knew? I should be in the company of like-minded people, they decided. Sridhar suggested that I join a club which met in Lal Bagh every morning.

'What does the club do?' I had asked suspiciously.

'This is a laughing club, Appa', Sridhar replied enthusiastically. For his sake, I joined the club. A whole lot of old buffoons laughing like morons early in the morning. It made me surlier.

When the laughing club idea failed, my family conspired to put me in some new-fad spiritual course. They thought meditation will help calm me down. For that nonsense course also I went, just to keep peace. The instructor said I can't have coffee during the course. I did not go back. Damn you people with your rules, rules, rules, I had thought darkly.

It did not take long for my family to give up on me. Slowly, I realized whenever I was in the room, a hush fell, or the conversation would be polite and guarded. I wanted to laugh with them and participate in their lives, but I had isolated myself. Why had this happened?

We reached the wedding hall. Sharada was immediately encircled by a group of ladies of all ages, shapes and sizes and whisked away. Yes. No function could proceed smoothly without Sharada's expertise. I was left behind, seated amidst other such left-over husbands. These idiots could talk only about two things—either kidney problems or my retirement.

'These small-time showrooms will definitely need cashiers. With your accountant background, you will easily get some part-time job', Badri said. He is a misshapen clown with a finger always exploring his nose. Misshapen because his belly is abnormally huge compared to the rest of his body—like a *ghatam* tied around a bamboo stick. This is because almost every day of the year he eats in some function or the other—marriage, naming ceremony, *upanayanams* or, if nothing is there, then he'll attend some *thithi*. I don't even know how we are related, but he's always there in all the functions, acting as if he was Veda Vyasa's son-in-law.

'No! No!' someone replied. I did not recognise this fool, but I knew his type—self-styled astrologer for sure. 'Again working as cashier and all that is stressful', he drawled in an all-knowing tone. 'Seshadri, do you know that small Ganapati temple two roads away from your house?'

I grunted a yes. Who was this fellow and why did he know my name and where I lived? All the veins in my body started to throb. The *mangalya* ceremony was long over, and it was nearing one in the afternoon. Yet, there was no sign of announcing lunch in this blasted marriage ceremony. The priest was a slow cow. I wanted to jump into the mandap and whack his head just to speed things up. He did not even know the mantras properly, kept peeking into some torn book.

'Seshadri?' Astrologer fellow was looking at me with a my-advice-is-great smile.

'I did not hear', I replied. My frown had deepened.

'I said you can work in that Ganapati temple. Just be a part of the trust and oversee temple management. The environment will suit your personality.'

'Why? WHAT? What do you THINK my personality is?' My voice was very high-pitched. Both fellows were taken aback. There was a lull in the conversation around me and people turned around to stare.

Astrologer-type meekly answered, 'No, what I meant was ... it will be nice to spend time in a temple. You will not get bored and make some money also ... .' He looked at Badri for support.

'I am not ninety. I AM ONLY SIXTY. I don't want to spend time in a temple. Anyway, it is none of your business. I will spend time watching MTV ... what is it to you?' I had not breathed.

Both fellows gaped at me. They just mumbled something to soothe me down. By then, I was like a Diwali rocket whose fuse had been lit. I got up pushing my chair back with a loud screech and stomped towards the mandap. Two old women were blocking the way; they were busy chatting.

'SIT DOWN AND YAK! CAN'T YOU SEE THE EMPTY CHAIRS?' I yelled. The shocked women scurried away like rabbits escaping a python. Now the noise in the wedding hall dropped to a murmur. I bet everyone was watching.

My next target was the priest. I marched up to the mandap and yelled at him too. He was so startled that he almost put his fat foot into the hissing and cackling *homa*. The bride and bridegroom looked at me, with thankful expressions, I must add. Soon, a bunch of elders calmed me down and chastised the priest for taking such a long time. Someone prudently escorted me to the dining hall and I ate in silence. I knew I had overstepped the limit that day. Creating a scene at a function like some low-class slum dweller. Anyway, I'd had enough of this wedding. I sought out Sharada and told her I was leaving. Of course she had seen my performance.

'I will come back with Sridhar, after the reception. You ... you don't worry. There is dosa batter in the fridge for your evening tiffin.'

Had Sharada been angry, perhaps I would not have felt miserable. Instead, there was so much sadness in her eyes, so much despondent worry about me, that it broke my heart. I was letting her down, I knew it. It seemed as if I was unable to stop myself ... hurtling down this path of self-destruction.

I decided to walk back home. Outside, the sunny morning had turned into a grey afternoon, darker than my temper. As I walked, the wind picked up speed; waste plastic covers and other rubbish rose in the air like kites. Dust swirled around my feet. There were no warning drops. The skies burst open thunderously and the rain came in sheets.

I had just about reached one of the by-lanes in Jayanagar. I quickly hopped into a doorway, but not before getting considerably wet. I wiped my face and head as best as I could with a wet handkerchief. Well, there was nothing to do but to stand and watch the rain. This was the kind of monsoon rain that Bengaluru dreaded—it was the flooding rain. It wouldn't stop for another two hours, at least. I thought of the people all cosy and warm in the wedding hall. I looked at myself, shivering like a wet cat, stranded on the street. Of course I was to blame, and I could not understand why. I felt a hollow in my stomach, a painful pinch in my chest, and before long, I was crying as fitfully as the sky.

I was startled when I heard a cough. I turned around. There was a flight of stairs behind me, disappearing into a dimly lit landing. On the landing, I saw an elderly gentleman, possibly my age.

'Please, do come up and make yourself comfortable. It will be a while before the rain stops', his voice was soft.

I nodded and went up the stairs.

'This way', he smiled and pointed to an open corridor on the first floor. The corridor was lined by what seemed like shops—all with their shutters down.

'All these shops are vacant ... some dispute', my host informed me as we reached the end of the corridor and stood in front of a clinic. I looked up at the board; it said, 'Happiness Clinic'. What a ridiculous name, I thought. But out of politeness I said, 'So you are a doctor, sir?'

My host nodded and smiled. 'Come inside', he invited.

It was a relief to step inside, even though it was just a flimsy plywood partition that marked the 'inside'. A wooden bench and two wooden stools were the only furniture. The doctor's practice did not look all that prosperous. The peeling plaster on one of the walls was held together by a huge chart showing different parts of the brain. I was about to sit on the bench when the doctor said, 'I have better seating arrangements in the consultation area ... come in, come in.'

The consultation room was indeed very comfortable. The ferocious noise of the rain receded to a gentle murmur inside. It was not a very large room—perhaps ten feet by eight. A table with the doctor's journals and other paraphernalia was set at the far end of the room. A large part of the room was taken up by two comfortable sofas facing each other, separated by a coffee table. There was no examination table too. This was certainly different from the clinics I had been to, and I told the doctor as much.

'I am a psychologist', the doctor said, as he strode towards a cabinet near his table. He retrieved a towel from a drawer and gave it to me. 'Sit down, sit down. Make yourself comfortable. Nasty weather today.'

I accepted the towel gratefully.

'Sit down, please', the doctor pointed to the sofa. He walked back to his desk and retrieved two Styrofoam cups and a steel flask. Soon we were comfortably seated; a very strong ginger tea was warming my bones.

The doctor switched on a portable tube light. 'There, that's better.'

I smiled. We made some small talk about the rain and infrastructure in Bengaluru. I realised that for the first time in two years, I was having a pleasant conversation with another adult. The doctor was a lean, tall man. Lean but very fit; there was certain vitality about him. His hair was rich silver, swept back neatly, softening his angular face. Perhaps in his youth, when that silver was black, his features would have been sharper.

'By the way, I am Seshadri', I introduced myself. I wanted to give a handshake, but for that, I had to get up from the comfortable sofa. I remained put—let him only extend his hand.

'Oh! This is such a coincidence! My name is Seshadri too!' The doctor smiled enthusiastically like a small boy. He did not extend his hand.

We fell into easy conversation. Eventually, there was one of those comfortable lulls. After much hesitation, I said, 'Doctor, I want some advice.'

'Tell me.'

I stared at the empty cup. 'I mean ... please don't think I am wheedling out a free session. I ... '

'No ... no, Seshadri. Just go ahead.'

'I think I am suffering from some kind of depression.'

'Go on.'

I took a deep breath and began. 'I was never like this. But for last two years, something has changed inside me. I have become irritable, I lose my temper very quickly, I can't get along with people ... I feel ... I feel everyone is out to get me. I am always afraid something bad will happen to Sharada ... my wife. I suffer from insomnia ... and sometimes, as I lie awake, I check on Sharada's breathing ... you know ... .' There was a shake in my voice.

'Was there any incident that triggered this?' The doctor's voice was calm and reassuring.

I dreaded telling him about my retirement. I did not want him say 'Aha it is the retirement!' But I decided to be honest anyway.

'I retired two years ago. Although the timelines coincide, I am sure it has nothing to do with my retirement. I don't regret my retirement. I was just so relieved that my mechanical life was done. I did not enjoy my job anyway—it was just that. A job.'

'Tell me more about your state of mind.'

'I just feel suffocated ... mentally suffocated all the time.'

'Go on. Don't hold back any thought. Speaking your thoughts aloud has a strange power.'

I sat quietly for a minute, choosing words and arranging sentences in my mind. I had an overwhelming sense of urgency; somehow it was very important this stranger understand me.

'I am sixty-one', I began, staring at the floor. 'Assuming I will live for another twenty years, I feel this ... this panic. I have only ... maybe ... ten years of productive life left, in which I have to cram all the things I want to do. From that, two years have gone down the drain ... because ... I ... I don't know what I want to do. I don't know who I am. I feel so frustrated because ... I don't have any identity. Do you also think this is a natural after-effect of retirement?'

'No', the doctor said without any hesitation. I was relieved. 'What you are saying is something deeper. Tell me more about your family life. Your relationship with your parents, wife, children.'

I shrugged. 'I had a normal childhood. Very loving home. I am the only son, so obviously my parents doted on me. Gave me a good education; I got a job, got married, had a son ... and now I am here. My wife is everything one could wish for in a spouse. I am very proud of my son. He is now married.'

'Hmm. You specifically spoke of identity. Something has wounded you. And the wound goes back to your childhood—or perhaps youth at least. Want to talk about it?'

I gave a nervous laugh. 'There is nothing in my life that I've done which was a result of my own decision. Even ... even marrying Sharada. It was an arranged marriage—it is another matter that I fell in love with her the minute I saw her', I smiled at the memory. 'But, god forbid, had I not liked Sharada, even then I would have married her. Because she was my parents' choice.'

I looked up at the doctor. 'I don't want to come across as someone who is ungrateful to his own parents ... '

The doctor waved his hand. 'Disagreement, differing opinions, these are not signs of disrespect. It only means you are a healthy, thinking individual. Tell me more. What does identity mean to you?'

Buoyed by the doctor's words, I laid bare my thoughts— thoughts that I often perceived as dark and sinful. 'For forty-five years, my identity was that I was an accountant. Did I want to be an accountant? I can't even remember. You see, all my life, I have done what my father wanted me to do. "Seshadri, you will study commerce. Seshadri, you will go to this college. Seshadri, you will join this job. Seshadri, you will build a house here." I felt I was always in a cocoon. Lines were drawn for me everywhere. It offered me a sense of security. Looking back, I feel I've just existed. Do you understand what I am saying?' I looked at the doctor intently.

'Yes. Perfectly.'

'As long as I was within the line, life would go on smoothly', I continued. 'This constant hammering of what to do, when to do, how to do ... well ... it has driven out all confidence in me. I have always lived by the rules. Now, my parents are no more. My job is no more. So those boundaries are gone. And all I see is emptiness. It is not about filling time. I mean ... whether I am busy throughout the day, or whether I choose to just sit and stare at the wall, the hours fly by. The day is over. Another day starts. Around me, people's lives also go on. Sridhar has his office. Sharada has her cooking and cleaning routine. I mean whether I am there or not ... it does not make a difference. I ... I feel like a man stranded on a highway ... you know ... all around me, everyone is travelling at high speed but I am standing still. So to answer your question, I don't know what identity stands for. Who am I? I don't know.'

'There are really two aspects to what you are saying. One', the doctor counted on his fingers, 'you are trying to find yourself. You are not an accountant, you are no longer a son, and as a father and husband, your role has diminished. Two, you have stored years and years of resentment, even without your knowledge. All these years, your other roles and duties filled up your mind, and now, when your primary roles have reduced, the resentment has resurfaced.'

'Yes', I nodded. 'Yes, you are so right.'

'Have you discussed this with your wife?'

'No. Poor thing, she is already troubled by my behaviour. She is a simple soul, doctor. She won't understand these complex things I am going through.'

'If there is anyone who can understand your situation, Seshadri, it is your wife. You are facing this now. She has been facing it all her life.'

I looked at the doctor, my famous irritation flaring up. Is he out of his mind?

'Like you, what choices did she have?' the doctor asked. 'It is even worse for her. She was what ... maybe twenty ... twenty-one when she got married? Yes? Imagine her bewilderment. At that young age, she had to steel her mind to putting her life in the hands of a stranger. Unlike you, she did not even have the choice to go out in the world, isn't it? Who knows? She may have had the potential to be a very capable leader, a visionary industrialist or even a successful entrepreneur. But our society nips this potential in the bud. She was just moved from one house to another. She was to adopt this new family as her own. All at the tender age of twenty. It is daunting, Seshadri. And that is why—no one on Earth can understand your anguish better than her.'

I was stunned to silence. I had never given this a thought. 'This is the way things have always been in our society', I mumbled defensively.

The doctor nodded. 'The difference is ... in her case, as with many women, when there are no options at all, they make the best of whatever situation they are thrust in. They create a new world; they generate their own happiness. Generate, mind you, not find. This mental imprisonment is the greatest tragedy of our society. Instead of correcting it, we glorify it. That is the second tragedy.'

'I ... I don't know what to say', I replied.

'We are all victims of this system. But it's never too late to start on a new path, yes? So let us try two things. First, we should get rid of your resentment.'

'How, doctor?' my voice trembled. 'If anything, my agony has increased.'

'Seshadri', the doctor leaned forward. 'Think of an old closet. Let us say, for many years you have been dumping unwashed laundry into this closet. For forty years, you never remove anything from here, but you only keep adding. You keep this closet locked all the time. What do you think will happen whenever you open the door?'

I was quiet. What was he getting at? 'The stink will be unbearable', I said.

The doctor nodded. 'Let us say you want to clean this closet. How will you do it?'

I shrugged. 'I will throw out all the stinking clothes ... in fact, burn them. Disinfect the closet and keep the doors open for fresh air. Keep it in some sunshine.'

'Exactly', the doctor clapped his hands. 'The mind is like a closet, Seshadri. All these negative emotions like fear, bad memories, anger, hatred, jealousy ... these are like dirty laundry. We humans tend to nurture these feelings and feel sorry for ourselves. Before long, we would have collected so much dirty laundry that our mind starts to stink. This negativity takes over our personality ... it spreads like a dark ink drop blotting on a tissue paper. What happens when you touch an ink-smudged paper? It rubs off on your skin, right? It is the same with a person with only negative thoughts. This person's negativity rubs around everywhere, making everyone unhappy. It is like looking out of a window, through a very dirty pane, stained with years of dust and dirt. No matter how beautiful the view, you will always see the world as a dirty place.'

Deep down, I knew he was right.

'Open your closet', the doctor gestured. 'Let sunshine illuminate every dark corner. Throw out all these negative feelings. Throw out the frustrations of your adulthood. They serve no purpose. Instead, like rot, they will weaken you.'

I could not help but smile. Outside, the rain had stopped; I could now hear the murmur of traffic.

'The second thing ... the most important thing you need to do is to talk to your wife. When I say talk, I actually mean communicate. Listen to her. Allow her to talk. In her words, you will find yours.'

I nodded and stood up.

The doctor stood up too. 'You are always welcome here—drop in around this time on any day ... I am always free.'

I thanked him over and over again and promised to meet him in a couple of days.

I hurried back home, hardly feeling the ground below me. I felt light and uplifted. I turned into my street, and was touched to see that Sharada was standing by the gate, looking up and down the road. I could see Sridhar pacing around too.

Sharada opened the gate as soon as I neared the house. 'Where had you gone?' her face and voice crumpled. 'Don't you have any sense? Don't you realise how worried we all are?'

Had I not met the doctor, Sharada's outburst would've drawn out a loud and angry retort from me. But today, I just smiled. I only saw love in her anger.

'Sorry, Sharadu', I said meekly. 'I met a friend and lost track of time.'

Sharada looked relieved and surprised at my reaction. She grumbled about me going hungry, held my hand and almost dragged me inside. 'Don't stir out of my eyesight', she said, her eyes glistening.

'I won't. Now give me something to eat. I am famished.'

It was a pleasant evening—something I'd not experienced for a long time. After Sridhar left, I awkwardly started my conversation with Sharada. Hesitantly, at first, as if I were talking to a stranger, and then, the words came out in a deluge. We spoke late into the night. Yes, we had been husband and wife for more than four decades, but that night, we became soulmates.

As I listened to Sharada, I realised what a small man I'd been. Sharada has a distinction in M.Sc. Mathematics. How easily I had brushed it aside all these years—not just me, but all of us, my family, her family. Her accomplishment was so insignificant in all our eyes; her degree was just a piece of paper. For me, I had found the ideal wife who would keep my family happy. For her parents, her degree ensured she got a good husband. The doctor was right. She, like other women, was just moved from one house to another.

'I will not pretend and say I was happy and this was an ideal sacrifice', Sharada confessed. 'When you educate a person, it is not just about learning something, no? In that process the person also realises her own worth—intelligence, capabilities. So when you are told it is all inconsequential, you are only destined to be a wife and mother—it is heartbreaking.'

I could say nothing; I felt ashamed. I merely held her hand.

'But I have no regrets. Yes, it was my ambition to become a teacher. I am sure it would have been workable—we have so many schools nearby. But you only know what the situation was in the family, right?'

I nodded. Both my parents were paralytic, requiring round-the-clock care. Sharada herself had undergone two miscarriages before Sridhar was born.

'Anyway', Sharada smiled. 'I won't say my degree went for a waste. Many of Sridhar's classmates came to me for tuitions. Of course I would not take money ... but you know ... all my students are now in big-big posts. Particularly Prakasha—

you remember that nurse who used to come home to help me with Appa and Amma? Her son. I taught him from third standard right through to his PUC. I coached him for his IIT entrance also. You know now where he is?' Her face glowed.

I still did not find my voice—I was shrinking into myself. She did not wait for an answer. 'He is in ISRO. He is a part of the PSLV core team.'

I looked at her proud smile, her radiant face and remembered the doctor's words about generating happiness. That's what Sharada had done. I would have withered away in her situation. A brilliant mind reduced to giving bedpans during the best part of her youth. But she did not play a victim like I'm doing now. She did not wait for someone to handover happiness on a tray. She chose to generate her happiness.

'So when you say you are trying to find yourself—I completely understand', she said softly.

It was gurkha-hour by the time we turned in. As I lay in bed, listening to Sharada's snores, all my anxieties and fears melted and came out through my eyes. A new fire seized me, even as I was being purified by my tears. I had to give back Sharada her life. I did not know how, in what form, but amends had to be made. Only by that act could I redeem myself, find myself, define myself.

Over the next couple of days, there was a transformation in me that stunned everyone, including myself. The lethargy, the irritation, the feeling of emptiness and helplessness ... all had vanished without a trace.

For some reason, I did not tell anyone about my encounter with the doctor. He was my special secret. I met him almost every day. We'd have long chats—some philosophical, some psychological— and each day, I would return enriched by his knowledge.

One evening, the doctor was reading out an article about a nonagenarian marathoner. 'Seshadri, he also has two legs and two hands like us. At ninety plus, physically he must be weaker than us. Still ... he has done something that ninety percent of us can't do. You know why?'

I just leaned back and smiled. The doctor usually answered his own questions. He tapped his forehead and said, 'It's all in the mind, Seshadri. That is the difference. The power of thought.'

Just then, a noise outside the clinic disturbed us. Before we could react, the door to the inner consultation area was yanked open, and a surprised kid tumbled in. He was about ten years old, dressed in a black and grey checked shirt and black shorts with Spiderman printed on the pockets. He yelped in a startled way when he saw us.

'Do you want to meet Doctor Uncle?' I asked with a smile.

The boy looked frightened—he looked around and looked at me. He shook his head and ran away.

I laughed and turned to the doctor. I could see that our train of thought was broken and we sat in comfortable silence. I eventually took leave, promising to meet him as usual.

I pondered over the doctor's words as I walked home. *Thoughts have power. The mind makes a difference.* If a ninety-year-old can run a marathon, what is to stop my young Sharada from pursuing her teaching ambition?

Instead of heading home, I walked to Rajanna's library two streets away from my home.

Rajanna was also like me—old timer in that area, pushing seventy. He had retired as a librarian in a government college. He also lived in a housing board allotment, like mine. He was a widower and lived alone; his three children lived outside Bengaluru. He had converted one of the bedrooms in his house into a circulating library. The only things that circulated in his library were air and dust.

He was surprised to see me. 'Came to borrow a book?' his smile was almost toothless.

'No', I said. 'I have something important to discuss with you.' I planned to ask him for some contacts in the government college where he'd worked. Surely, someone can appoint Sharada in a temporary post? Even if it was a small school—it would be worth it.

But our discussion went in another direction. We spoke for more than two hours. By the end of it, I was jubilant. When we parted, Rajanna and I were business partners.

'Sharadu, I want you to get back into teaching. Full time', I said when I reached home, even before I'd left my footwear near the door.

Sharada laughed. 'Which duffer college is looking for an inexperienced, old woman to teach? And I should start a career at this age, is it? No need.'

'Sit down, I will explain', I said, holding her hand and dragging her to the sofa.

'You know Library Rajanna? He is sitting and swatting flies ... wearing torn *jubba* and *panche*. He had plans of expanding his library in the terrace. So he put up a Teflon roof with those aluminium frames and sliding windows. He spent more than seventy-five thousand for that.'

'*Aiyoo!*' Sharada's hands went up to her ears. 'All his savings, is it?'

'Yes. He gets a pension of two thousand rupees per month. He is living on that only now. He will not take money from his children. He still thinks his library will run; it is going slow because he is not able to advertise. That's what the fool says.'

'So what is your plan?'

'I told him I will pay rent for the terrace. Sharadu, you can start Maths tuitions there. Free classes. So you can create more Prakashas. I convinced Rajanna to stock textbooks. So his library also will run. I will help him in procuring more books and keeping a tab on the library. What do you say?'

She did not have to say anything. Her face, her smile, the way she held my hand told it all.

I printed some pamphlets and asked the local newspaper man to distribute it in the nearby streets.

We initially got fifteen enrolments—all students from poor families, the parents being vegetable vendors or domestic help. It was good enough for us. Sharada grouped the kids based on their knowledge level and drew up a tuition schedule. Seeing her interacting with the children, specs perched on her nose, writing in her notebook—my heart swelled with pride. It was like watching a rare flower bloom.

We fixed on a date to commence the tuitions. I got busy shopping stationery for Sharada—exercise notebooks for the kids, a white board, markers, charts and whatnot. I got a sign board painted—it said Sharada Tutorials. Below that, I had 'free classes' painted in italics. The sign board boy also enrolled—he was to appear for SSLC board exams that year.

Sharada's classes started, and within a week, the enrolment had doubled. Sharada was now busy throughout the day. She handled degree students early in the morning and late in the evening. The little ones would come in the afternoon.

Soon, Sharada's free time went in creating new lessons and correcting papers. I realised Sharada was a brilliant teacher. Her approach was different; she made Maths creative. Now, whenever I walked to the market, people called me as 'Sharada Madam's mister'. I felt proud. Invariably, someone would come up to me and hand over some vegetables and say, 'For Sharada Miss.' Sometimes, a maid would turn up and clean the house for free.

It was almost a month since I'd been to the doctor. I was bursting to tell him about all these developments—after all, he was responsible for these changes. It was funny; we had become quite close friends, yet, I did not know his last name, where he lived or his telephone number. I hurried to his clinic one afternoon, intent on inviting him home and showing him Sharada Tutorials. It was 2 p.m. but I hoped he would be in the clinic. As far as I knew, he did not consult anywhere else.

I reached the doorway to Happiness Clinic and almost ran up the stairs. When I reached the corridor, I stopped short and gasped. The series of shops on this floor stood in ruins. There were bricks and jelly stones lying everywhere. I ran towards the clinic. It stood in shambles too. Gone were the rickety benches, the comfortable chairs. I was distraught. I cursed myself for not being in touch with this wonderful man. Where did my friend go?

In panic, I hurried back to the road. There was a small provision store opposite this building. I dashed across and peered inside. The owner of the store was an old man. He was dressed in a torn vest and lungi. He was reading a Kannada daily, the paper ruffled by an ancient table fan that whirred reluctantly. It was one of those small *kirana* shops where you could buy everything—from noodles to notebooks. He looked up and removed his thick glasses.

'That opposite building', my voice was shrill, 'when was it demolished?'

The shopkeeper peered out. 'It has been like that forever.'

My expression must have alarmed him. He came out of his shop and stood next to me. He pointed to the building and said, 'That one?'

I nodded.

'Yes … it has been under litigation for a long time. More than twenty years, I think. I have been here all my life, and as far as I can remember, it has always been like this.'

There must be some horrible mistake! I must have come to the wrong place. But how can that be? I had spent so many evenings in this very same building.

'There was a clinic called Happiness Clinic in that building. Do you know where it is? There was a doctor … hmmm … my age, tall … have you seen him?'

'No, you must have come to the wrong road.' The shopkeeper stared at me.

I mumbled my thanks and left. I had walked a couple of paces when I spotted the kid who had rushed into the clinic during one of my discussions with the doctor. The kid was playing by himself with a bunch of marbles on the footpath. A lady, presumably his mother, sat nearby cleaning ragi.

I called out to the kid. 'No school today?'

The kid looked at me hesitantly. 'Go on! Give an answer to *thaatha*', his mother cajoled him.

'I had been to school in the morning', the boy replied shyly, twisting his shirt tail.

I turned to the child's mother and asked her about the building.

'You must have come to the wrong road, saar', she replied. 'We have been living here for last five years … that building has always been in ruins.'

I just nodded and looked at the kid. He had stopped playing and was staring at me. I looked back at the mother. She was now busy talking to a neighbour.

'You have seen me with Doctor Uncle, right? Do you know where Doctor Uncle is?' I spoke to the kid in an urgent, low voice.

The kid continued to stare at me. Eventually, when I was about to move on, he said, 'You were alone.' He addressed me in a singular term, in the unabashed manner in which kids speak. I turned to him … perhaps I had not heard him correctly?

'You were alone', the kid repeated. 'Speaking to yourself. Every time you went into that building, I followed you. You would sit on a broken chair and talk to yourself. I thought you were practicing for a drama. Afterwards, I got bored.' The boy went back to playing with his marbles.

Cold sweat seeped out of my pores and my breath came in short gasps. I hurried home, lest I faint on the road. Who was that doctor? Did I imagine him? He said his name was Seshadri too ... did I have a split personality? Or had I spent the best days of my life with a ghost? Or, was it God who came in the form of a friend to help me? Perhaps I was so depressed and frustrated that I had projected my own sub-conscious mind? I will never know the answers to these questions for the rest of my life.

Days rolled into months and life went on. I missed my friend in a deep way, whoever or whatever he was. He had protected me. Changed my life. Whenever I saw a shock of silver hair, my pulse quickened. Sometimes I'd wake up from a dream, his voice echoing in my head. A part of me never stopped seeking him out. For now, his imprint is visible in Sharada's success, in the never-ending queue of students who come to touch her feet and proudly show their results.

Tomorrow, these children will become engineers, businessmen, research analysts and spread all over the globe. I pacify myself—the Happiness Clinic will live on through them.

# BEST FRIENDS FOREVER

My evening shift was done. The paperwork waited in colour-coded ring files, but that could be ignored for a couple of hours. I laced up my ASICS in a hurry. The deer would have already come out to the lake, and it was a two kilometre jog to the spot. I loved to watch them line up at the edge of the water, their reflections perfectly symmetrical in the still air of this place.

The Nisarga Psychiatric Research Centre stands at the head of the Rishi *keré* or lake, fed by the Kabini reservoir in H. D. Koté taluk. Set on a ten-acre plot, the hospital is a cluster of buildings housing psychiatric units, labs and administration offices. I'm glad they did not go for a high-rise architecture and chose this unobtrusive design instead, blending into the virgin beauty of the area. There is also a group of cottages at the far end of the property—staff accommodation and guest houses for family members of patients. All this is enclosed in high compound walls, with the lake lapping the east wall.

On the opposite bank of the lake, the Kakanakote forest looms in a green-black mass, with its secret thrumming language. In the evenings, when the water turns liquid gold, I could watch deer, sometimes even elephant herds, draw their fill from the lake.

I joined Nisarga five years ago as a senior psychiatrist. I had a choice of working in their main hospital unit in Bengaluru, but the recruitment panel strongly recommended I consider moving to H. D. Koté, since my core expertise was in the area of psychiatric research. Although the H. D. Koté campus is primarily a research centre, it took in resident patients with severe forms of mental illnesses.

I had my misgivings initially; after all, the facility was completely out of the high-power networking circuit. The one that Bengaluru or New Delhi could offer. Yeah, I could have chosen Bengaluru. Presented papers in stuffy conferences overseas, hobnobbed with fat old farts to climb the career ladder and so on. Perhaps I would have done that if Shabnam and I had not drifted away.

I met Shabnam as a research student in the Institute of Psychiatry in King's College, London. She specialised in addictions, while I majored in psychosis studies. Our courtship was wild and intense, like the turbulent birth of a river. But we settled down; our love had found its level and we revelled in the placidity. We returned to India with doctorates, struggled in unsatisfying jobs and often spoke of setting up something on our own. But I was a researcher at heart, and I was unsure of floating any venture. Eventually, she got a good position in AIIMS, New Delhi, while I stayed back in NIMHANS in Bengaluru. The relationship had run its course, though we did love each other. Only, it was no longer the imprisoning love that demanded two people sleep next to each other under the same roof. She found someone else, and now has two cherubs. There is no awkwardness between us, only a warm, spiritual connection. All the awkwardness was supplied by family and friends.

I'd only perceived beauty, luminous intelligence and a touching social commitment in Shabnam, but my family drew a picture of her based only on her religion. They made their relief apparent. I am not blaming them ... I mean ... I know how these emotions run. Even so, the melodrama depressed me. My friends, on the other hand, behaved as if I had a terminal disease because I'd 'lost' Shabnam; as if she were an expensive mobile phone or credit card.

Suffice to say the offer from Nisarga was serendipitous. Sure, the research facilities were the best I'd seen, but honestly, I accepted the offer because it provided the social isolation I craved for. Also, I fell in love with the place utterly. Now, I can't stay in any city for more than a day or two at a stretch.

My mobile phone pinged, alerting me to an SMS. It was Nagraj, head of security. He always texted me when he spotted the deer on his CCTV—'ur frenz r alrdy here.'

I shoved my access card into my pocket and was about to leave when my phone rang. It was my direct line.

'May I speak to Dr Srinidhi Krishnamurthy please?' The voice on the other end was slightly high-pitched, almost like a little girl's.

'This is Dr Srinidhi.'

'Oh good. Doctor, my name is Prerna. I want to check myself into Nisarga. Like … now. I … I had a terrible panic attack. I need help. I want to be put under observation.'

I frowned at my wristwatch. It was ten minutes past seven. 'Prerna, I want to know where you are right now, and if you are safe.'

'I stay in Bengaluru. Yes I'm okay now … I'm with my parents. I had the attack two days ago, but I'm afraid I'll have more.'

'Prerna, I think you meant to call the Nisarga Hospital in Bengaluru. Give me your number. I will immediately get an appointment for you and call you back.'

'No! I want to come to Nisarga in H. D. Koté.'

'This is a research facility, Prerna. We take in patients only with … huh … advanced mental illnesses. Trust me, I can arrange for a consultation immediately for you.'

Prerna gave a high-strung laugh that pushed an alarm button inside my head. 'Oh believe me. I'm quite advanced in the mental illness department. We have already started for Nisarga, doctor. We are almost near H. D. Koté Hand Post. I will sit at the gates of your hospital till you take me in. But it has to be Nisarga. Has to! Has to!'

'I'll keep all the paperwork ready for your admission, Prerna', I said in a low voice, calming her down instantly. This was the strangest call I'd ever attended to. 'Who is travelling with you?'

'My parents.'

'I will arrange for their accommodation too. I will see you in an hour or so? Okay?'

I only heard a sob in response.


Prerna arrived around eight thirty. Her admission formalities were completed quickly. She was a petite twenty-seven-year-old. She looked like a high school kid in her pixie haircut, scruffy jeans and a tee shirt with Jimi Hendrix's face printed on it.

'You know, I'd started a Jimi Hendrix fan club back in college', I smiled at her. I wanted to assess how keyed up she was. 'Are you a fan too?'

She smiled unsurely and nodded, a feather of her short hair

springing up in the gesture. As I filled out her forms, she stood in the middle of the reception area, looking around, almost gaping. Her parents looked on warily.

We accompanied Prerna to her ward, a cosy and cheerful room. Her parents looked around surprised.

'Nisarga is unlike other hospitals', I said. They were probably expecting white linoleum tiles everywhere, smelling of disinfectants. They did not reply. Not even a smile.

'I'd like to call it a day', Prerna said, clambering onto the bed. 'I will talk to you tomorrow, doctor.'

'Yes, of course. I have to inform you that this room is monitored by CCTV. The doctor on duty will be checking on you every hour.'

She shrugged in response.

'I will stay in her room, of course', her mother said in a challenging tone.

'I'm sorry ... we don't allow family members to sleep in the same room as the patients.' I firmly led Prerna's parents away.

The next morning, before I met Prerna, I briefly interviewed her parents to get a background on her case. I was curious about her insistence on Nisarga. She seemed fine, but high-strung. I intended to keep her here for a day or two, just to calm her down. Besides, the accommodation for family members was expensive considering Nisarga was a private hospital.

'Prerna has grown up in these parts', her father Ashwath Rajanna said. He was a tall man, ramrod straight. 'We are worried that coming back here will trigger some memories. We did our best to persuade her to see someone in Bengaluru itself, but she became very frantic ... like ... her life depended on coming here.'

'Did she have any traumatic experience here?'

Rajanna cleared his throat a couple of times. But it was Prerna's mother, Susheela, who answered.

'When Pammi ... Prerna was five, we had moved from Bengaluru to ... ' Susheela looked at her husband and continued, 'to H. D. Koté. So Pammi became a bit lonely, I think. She had to leave her friends behind ... it must have been stressful. She started bedwetting. It went on till she was almost ten. She had made up an imaginary friend. She started talking to this friend at all times of day and night ... even if people were around her. Finally we took her to a child psychologist. Not that it helped ... but by the time she hit her teens, the problem disappeared. By then we were also back in Bengaluru.'

'There was no problem once we moved to Bengaluru', Rajanna said. 'I mean she had a very normal adolescence, excelled in her studies, got a good job ... '

'Yes, yes', Susheela nodded vigorously. 'In fact, she had forgotten about that imaginary friend completely. Then suddenly ... ' Her face crumpled.

I handed a tissue box to the sobbing lady and offered her a glass of water. She recovered after a couple of minutes and continued, 'Suddenly, two days ago we got a call from her office. They said something happened to Pammi and the resident doctor had to sedate her. We brought her back home. When she woke up ... she was again talking to the air. She told us her imaginary friend was back.'

'Was there any specific incident that triggered this hallucination?'

'No ... nothing that we know of. Maybe work pressure? She has been under a lot of stress lately. Working late and not eating properly.'

'Did Prerna seem withdrawn ... you know, socially and emotionally? Over a period of, say, last six months to one year?'

'Oh no', Prerna's father smiled. 'Pammi and withdrawn? Never. Once she starts talking, uff! You will bow before her and beg for one minute's silence. She has so many friends ... always they want Pammi. Movie means Pammi ... wedding means Pammi ... '

I nodded. 'Why did she insist on this place? Any idea?'

The couple kept quiet for a minute. Then Rajanna said, 'I think it's only fair that Pammi explains it to you.'

'Whatever is troubling Prerna, I'm sure we can help her', I reassured them. 'She has the support of a loving family and she comes across as a fighter, yes? Someone who holds the bull by the horns.'

Rajanna chuckled. 'You have no idea.'

'I will first have a couple of sessions with her. Depending on the evaluation, I might order some scans and tests. I may also bring on board an expert if need be. I will let you know.'

Five minutes into my first session with Prerna I realised that Rajanna was right—this girl was a motormouth. The minute I entered her room, she asked, 'What does insanity feel like?' She was sitting cross-legged on her bed, licking sambhar off her fingers each time she dunked a piece of dosa in it. The hospital gown dwarfed her and she looked like a child in a grown-up's clothes.

'I mean', she continued, 'from delusions to hallucinations, it seems I've progressed rapidly on the insanity scale. But I don't *feel* insane, you know?'

'We don't use the word "insane" here, Prerna.'

'Oh please. Let us not be politically correct. This is a loony bin. I'm still hungry.'

'Do you want another dosa?'

'I think I'll have *upma*.'

I rang for the ward boy and asked him to bring a plate of *upma* and two filter coffees.

'You were saying ... ' I prompted her.

'I mean ... I don't know how a mad person should feel. See, I can feel emotions. I can empathise. I make sense when I speak. I feel as normal as any twenty-seven-year-old. I've had my fair share of romances', she stopped to drink water. 'I enjoy sex', she balled a tissue after wiping her fingers and threw it into the bin with perfect aim. 'I can write perfectly good code in any programming language. Am I abnormal because I have visions? Or is the world abnormal because it cannot see my visions?'

I laughed. 'Whenever you are ready, we can talk about your visions.'

She looked at me for a minute. 'Aren't you kind of young to be a senior psychiatrist? I saw that on your name plate last evening. I thought you'll be ... like ... sixty or something. With specs. Maybe bald. Hair coming out of your ears.'

'Are you disappointed?' I asked with a serious face.

'Oh no. Surprised. So how old are you? I know it's obnoxious manners ... but ... I'm going to tell you a lot about my life ... so I may as well know.'

'I'm thirty-eight.'

'That's old', she said and immediately clapped her mouth shut. 'I'm so sorry, I did not mean to say that aloud', she mumbled.

'Does my age matter?' I asked, still keeping a straight face.

'No ... not really. You know I've met a psychologist as a kid? Hated that bastard.'

Not a start I was hoping for.

'You've been speaking to my parents, right? Did they tell you about ... about what happened back then?'

'No.'

'What did they tell you?'

'It's not important. I'm more interested in what you have to say.'

Prerna gave a wry smile. 'Bet they did not tell you I killed my grandmother.'

That came as a right hook. I was completely blindsided.

'Shall we start?' she said, leaning back on a stack of pillows.

'Of course. Our conversation will be videotaped. What you say will be absolutely confidential. I may discuss your case with experts if I feel the need for an advanced intervention. Okay?'

She shrugged and waited patiently as I fitted a wireless mike on her gown. The pulse on her neck jumped off my fingers as I fiddled with the clip. I set up the video equipment and recorded the patient details.

'Right. We are ready. But you can stop whenever you want to, okay?' I said as I pulled a chair by her bed, a notebook open on my lap.

She nodded. 'Why did they make this room so cheerful?'

I looked around and smiled. Indeed, none of the rooms in this wing resembled a hospital ward. This room looked more like a luxury cottage. Pink and blue butterflies dotted bright yellow walls. The curtains, the duvet, the cushions and even the coasters matched the walls.

'It's meant to cheer us loonies up, I suppose', Prerna said. 'It's quite a condescending decor. I hate this yellow ... it mocks my blue world.'

'Would you like to move to another room?'

'Oh no! No need for all that fuss', she waved her hand. 'I was just observing. I love this place actually. It's my home.'

'How so?'

'Because ... this was my home. Back when I was a kid.' Looking at my frown, she added, 'Oh this was not a hospital back then. All the other wings are new buildings. This wing', she patted the bed, 'this entire wing was our bungalow.'

'You mean you lived here?' I strained to keep the disbelief out of my voice. How did her parents miss telling me this important detail? Or, more importantly, why did they feel the need to hide this fact?

'I had to come back here', she said, adjusting the pillows. 'Anyway, let me get on. I guess it all started when I was five. We were in Bengaluru at that time. My father was a superintending engineer with Central Board for Irrigation and Power. It's a government undertaking. He was deputed on some irrigation projects here—across Kabini, Nugu and Taraka reservoirs. My mother worked for State Bank of Mysore. Initially it was decided that only my father would relocate because this was a long-term project. But when Ma visited the place, she fell in love with it. Going by his grade and seniority, they had allotted Papa this sprawling bungalow overlooking the Rishi keré. You can imagine right ... no high compound walls, no other buildings ... nothing. The bungalow stood in peaceful isolation. The other engineers were given quarters around H. D. Koté.

'In contrast, our house in Bengaluru was like a piece of handkerchief. Red oxide floors, chipped cement walls, rusty pipes and leaky taps. Anyway, Ma found out that she could get a transfer to the H. D. Koté branch easily. As far as my school was concerned, there was a private convent on the outskirts of H. D. Koté. Papa was given a government jeep to commute. So the jeep could drop me off to school, then Ma to her bank. It all fit in very well. We moved quickly.

'Till today, I've never lived in such a beautiful place. Beautiful, yet such painful memories. But I always had a romantic notion that I'd earn enough money to buy back this place and live here. Guess that's not possible now', she sighed.

'Anyway, this bungalow was built in the pre-independence era. Probably owned by one of those East India Company British officers. We found a lot of old photos and books. Looked like the owner was an important man, one Lord James Halliday—there were a lot of photos of him with the Wodeyar family. You know, having tea, playing golf, polo … that kind of stuff. It also looked like he had married an Indian lady. They had one daughter. At least we did not find photos of other children. Even in those sepia photos, it was hard not to miss the beauty of the woman and the daughter. A tiny scrawl on one of the photos identified them as Lady Harini Halliday nee Shanbogh and Miss Alice Halliday. The lady was dressed in what looked like Benaras silk in almost all the photos. The girl was in pretty frocks, reaching just above the knee, always in stockings and feet clad in buckled black shoes. Her waist-length hair was tied into a high pony tail in some photos. Ma figured the girl was probably eight or so. Me … I was besotted with the girl. She was the prettiest thing I'd ever seen. There was a water-colour portrait of hers, painted by her father. God … I should have saved all these things. Such an intimate part of my childhood. Anyway, Alice had inherited the beautiful features of her mother, but the light eyes and flaxen hair of her father. In the painting, her hair was loose, and fell to her waist like a golden veil. To me, she was like Rapunzel.

'I was no longer interested in Disney stories during bedtime. I wanted to hear about the Halliday family. I guess Ma was fed up with my incessant questions. She'd make up stories about the family … of all their wonderful adventures and travels. Soon, every time I kicked a fuss to drink my milk or eat my greens, Ma would take Alice's example. "Alice was such a good girl you know. She'd drink her milk before her mother could count to ten. That's why she always got first rank."

'"Where is Alice Ma?" I'd always ask.

'"She is back in England. The minute you grow big and strong, I will write to her and she will come to meet you." I guess I believed that rather thoroughly.

'I loved my new home and new life. We almost always had all our meals in the garden. I mean, imagine waking up in the morning and sitting in the garden for breakfast. And what do you see? All kinds of birds skimming on the golden lake. At the far end, deer would have just emerged from the forest. They'd totter up to the water and have their morning fill just as we had our coffee. You know, we have even seen crocodiles glide up to the banks. Especially in the summer.

'Trouble started with my Christmas vacations. My grand
mother—my father's mother—she called to say she'll be visiting
us. My vacations were starting, so Papa thought her timing was
perfect. Ajji ... what can I say ... she was a mean old woman. She
hated Ma because ... you know ... it was a love marriage. Although
Ma belonged to the same caste and all that, Ajji was unhappy and
never wasted an opportunity to hurl insults. When people told
her, you have a daughter-in-law who works in a bank, what more
you want, Ajji would retort, "A daughter-in-law who earns money
will dance on my head and treat me like a slave." Things got worse
when I was born. Ajji was of the opinion that had Papa married
the girl she had chosen after careful horoscope matching, I'd
have been a boy, and her husband's *vamsha* would have been safe.

'I suppose Ma and Papa argued a lot about inviting Ajji. Papa said
much time had passed, and we should relinquish the bitterness.
He wanted Ajji to have a chance to bond with me. Ma called Ajji a
foxy witch and a huge verbal duel erupted. Finally Papa managed
to convince Ma.

'Ajji came on the first weekend of my Christmas vacations.
Ma had prepared a feast. Ajji ate only curd-rice. "Are you out of
your head?" she scolded Ma. "In this age, how can I eat this *holige*
and *paaysa*? You have not made *saaru*, is it?" Poor Ma had made
*bisibelebath*. Later that afternoon, Ajji called her daughter, my
aunt, to say that she had reached safely and added dramatically
that after that long journey she was given only curd-rice because
the banker daughter-in-law did not have the common sense to
make *saaru*. And so it began.

'This bungalow has six bedrooms right ... all on the first floor.
This room where you put me in? This was our master bedroom.
Isn't it funny how you assigned me this room without knowing
any of these details?'

I nodded.

'Anyway', she continued, 'the ground floor had the kitchen,
a store room, a dining and a vast living room. Now the hospital
has converted the store room to your office. The dining room has
become a consultation area. Only the kitchen has been retained as
a cafeteria.

'So ... my parents had prepared a bedroom overlooking the

lake for Ajji. This room is two doors to the left. They thought she'll be very pleased.

'"Do you plan to kill me now only?" Ajji asked Papa. "How can I go up and down the stairs like this? Just give me a bed downstairs. I will sleep in the living room. Six rooms and see my karma? I have to sleep on the floor." So Papa called a couple of workers from the nearby village to move one of the cots from the upstairs bedroom down to the living room. Uneasy peace was restored.

'The next day, as my parents got ready for work, Ajji exploded. "So this is your plan. You want your old mother to run behind this monkey while your wife can put on lipstick and go to the bank swaying her butt?"

'Papa took a deep breath. "You only said you are very happy to come and stay with us. That you wanted to be with your granddaughter?"

'"Don't twist my words. I thought your wife will also take leave. Do you think I have the energy to cook and clean?"

'"You don't have to worry about that," Ma interrupted calmly. "Your breakfast, lunch and snacks ... everything is ready. A maid comes to clean the house. You just relax and play with Pammi."

'"*Che!* Her name is Prerna. Call her like that. Anyway eating what you have cooked ... only Shiva can save me."

'I cried when Papa and Ma were leaving for work. I felt very afraid of being alone with Ajji.

'"Nice drama you have taught this monkey," Ajji said.

'"I will come back early *bangara*," Ma said giving me a kiss.

'After they left, Ajji yanked me inside the house. "I have to do puja now. If I hear one small noise from you, I will tie you up in the forest, okay?"

I sobbed.

'"STOP CRYING," she yelled. "Sit on the sofa here. Don't move."

'I remember feeling hungry. So hungry. Ma always gave me a glass of milk before leaving for work. She had kept it on the dining table ... poor thing, she must have forgotten amidst the ruckus created by Ajji. I wanted to take it, but I was too afraid to move. Finally, I could not control my hunger and I tip-toed to the dining table. I could hear Ajji's murmur as she recited something. I had to drag a chair to reach the glass. The chair made a loud noise. Ajji's murmur stopped and she immediately came towards me. I screamed in fear and peed all over myself.

'"What did I tell you? Wait, I will get the ropes. I will tie you in the forest and all the lions and leopards will tear you up."

'I've never felt such black, abject fear as she dragged me. She opened the store room and shoved me inside. "I will lock you here for now. Wretched monkey. I have to wipe your urine and take bath again and start the puja again."'

I could see distress on Prerna's face. 'Do you want to take a break?' I asked her softly.

She shook her head. 'I heard the bolt being drawn. In a couple of minutes, I heard the water running. Trembling with hunger and fear, I curled up on the cold floor of the store room. It was a large room and still had many of the Halliday family stuff. Papa wanted to dispose them, but never got round to doing it. There were some old iron trunks, a broken rocking chair and musty smelling books.

'"Pammi ... Pammi ... wake up," a voice whispered. I felt a gentle pair of hands on my shoulders. I sat up and rubbed my eyes and stared. It was Alice! She looked exactly like in the portrait. Only more pretty.

'"Did you come from England?" I whispered.

'She shook her head. "This is my home. I live in a magic world, Pammi. Only you can see me!" She hopped in a funny way and clapped her hands. I smothered a giggle.

'"We both will be best friends, Pammi," she said and kissed both my cheeks.

'"I am very hungry," I said and cried a bit.

'"I can see Hanumakka coming to the house," Alice said, turning to the door. Hanumakka was our maid. "When she comes into the house, let us make a lot of noise here. She will then open the door for you. You can run out and have your milk. Tell Hanumakka you are hungry. She is carrying mangoes in her *butti*."

'In the next second, I heard Ajji opening the door for Hanumakka. Alice pointed at a brass vase. I held it over my head and threw it to the floor. It made satisfying noise. Hanumakka opened the storeroom door in a second. "Oh, it is you! I thought a big bandicoot has come inside the house."

'"I am hungry, Hanumakka," I cried and ran to her and clung to her legs. Hanumakka eyed Ajji who had returned to her *puja*. She carried me on her waist and fed me a glass of hot milk and biscuits.

'"Why are you smelling like this my dear," she asked in a low voice.

'I buried my head in her neck and cried inconsolably. Shame burned me.

'Hanumakka bathed me and helped me put on fresh clothes. "From tomorrow I will come early, my darling. I will stay as long as I can, okay?"

'My bedwetting started from that very day. The next few days were tolerable. Hanumakka, bless her pure soul, arrived before my parents left for work, and stayed till lunch time. She'd ensure I had my lunch before leaving. Anyway Ajji slept for three hours in the afternoon, and I would sit with Alice, listening to all her stories. Ma usually returned by the time Ajji woke up. The evenings invariably ended with Ajji complaining about something, and Ma going to bed crying.

'This continued for about two weeks. Then, Hanumakka had to go to the Malur fair so she took leave for two days. This incident happened on the day Hanumakka was supposed to return to work. She had sent word that she would come around noon. Ma had taken half a day off, so she promised to return by noon too. It meant I'd be alone with Ajji for a couple of hours. I did not mind, now that Alice kept me company. Besides, I knew Ajji's routine well enough to stay out of her way.

That day, I woke up early so Ma could help me with my bath—I was not allowed to go near hot water alone. I was done with my milk and tiffin by the time Amma left for the bank. Before Ajji could say anything, I ran upstairs. Alice was lying on my bed, reading one of my story books. "Come, let me tell you a story," she said.

'I guess I fell asleep because I did not hear Ajji come in. Alice shook me gently and placed a finger on her lips. She pointed at Ajji. Ajji's back was turned to us. She had opened Ma's cupboard and was rifling through all the sarees. "Thinks she is a movie star ... all costly-costly sarees," Ajji grumbled. Then she took out a pair of scissors that she'd tucked into her saree-fold at the navel.

'Alice sucked her breath. I knew what evil thing Ajji was about to do. "What are you doing?" I squealed and immediately clapped my mouth shut.

'Ajji turned around, furious. "Why you sneaky little devil! Pretending to be asleep but spying on me. Is this what your disgusting mother has taught you?"

'I started to cry.

'"If you tell anyone about this, you know what I will do?" She snipped the scissors menacingly. "I will chop your little, pink tongue." She advanced towards me in slow, deliberate steps. She tucked the scissors back in the saree and said, "Or maybe I will tie you in the forest."

'I cowered against the pillows, sobbing.

'Alice meanwhile screamed, "Leave her alone!" Of course, Ajji could not hear her. So Alice flung one of the story books at Ajji. It caught her on the lips and she staggered back; her eyes like saucers. Ajji had seen the book fly off by itself.

'She ran out of the room screaming. I could hear her telephone Papa. "Come home immediately. What? I don't care if your wife is on her way. You are the head of the family. Don't ask why ... just come!"

'I ran to the window as I heard a jeep pull up. That must be Ma! I sprinted downstairs just as Ma entered the house and flung myself at her, my body racked by my crying fit.

'My mother was terrified at my state. "What happened?" she asked Ajji. Ajji did not answer. She pushed aside Ma and walked outside.

'"I won't enter the house till my son comes. I don't know what harm you both will do to me."

'Papa came after twenty minutes. Before he could even speak, Ajji started wailing.

'"I was doing my puja and your daughter was playing upstairs. I became suspicious when I could not hear any noise. I knew she was up to no good. So I went upstairs to check. You know what she was about to do? She had a pair of scissors and was about to tear all of her mother's sarees. When I scolded her, she threw a book at my face. See?" She protruded her lower lip to show a non-existent injury.

'"Not just that. When I scolded her, she said she will chop off my tongue, the little devil."

'"ENOUGH!'" My mother's voice trembled with rage. "Don't you feel ashamed telling lies about a little child?" I hugged my mother's leg tightly. She lifted me and hoisted me on her waist.

'"How dare you talk to me like that? You are calling me a liar? Me?" Ajji thumped her chest like a chimpanzee.

'"Yes, you are a despicable liar. Do you think I don't know that you locked up the child in the store room? Hanumakka told me everything. You left this poor thing hungry. What kind of a woman are you?"

'"What?" Papa said, looking at Ma. "Locked up Pammi in the store room?"

'Ma narrated everything. "I just did not want to create a huge ruckus. Who knows what this woman is capable of? She might harm Pammi out of spite. I was anyway applying for leave ... to my bad luck, it got delayed."

'"She has wrapped you around your little finger. And you dance around like a clown," Ajji yelled at Papa.

'"I will put you on a bus back to Bengaluru right away. I won't even come to light your pyre. Go pack your bags. NOW!" I had never seen Papa so angry. Or Ma so livid for that matter. I had spasms of fear; I felt I was somehow responsible for all these fights. I felt afraid that after some time, the grownups would turn their anger to me. What if they left me in the forest?

'"Pammi's body is burning," Ma's voice cracked. "We have to take her to the doctor. Let me feed her something. It is noon and the poor darling has not eaten anything from morning."

'Alice was standing next to Ma all the while, holding my hand and kissing it repeatedly.

'Ajji refused to step inside the house. "Burn all my things if you want. I won't put even a toe inside your house."

'Papa turned around and marched to the almirah in the living room. He pulled out Ajji's sarees, balled them and threw them to the floor. Just then Hanumakka walked in. I guess she had heard all the screaming. She calmly told Papa, "I will take care of it, saar. You get the doctor first."

'Papa left in the jeep to get the doctor from Koté. Ma placed me on the sofa. "Pammi, you sit here darling. I will get your lunch. And today evening we can all have ice-cream!"

'"Can Alice also have ice cream, Ma?"

'"Of course! You ask Alice which ice-cream she wants."

'"Strawberry!" Alice squealed after Ma went away to the kitchen.

'My body felt very weak, as if it had been thrashed. I lay down and Alice started telling me the story of Snow White. Hanumakka finished packing Ajji's kit. She went to help Ma in the kitchen.

'Suddenly I was yanked by my shoulders. Ajji had a vice grip. She clamped my mouth shut with one hand and carried me swiftly out of the house. Alice screamed, but of course, no one heard her. I could see Alice over Ajji's shoulders. Alice did something strange. She kind of scrunched into a tight ball and expanded. The glass door of the almirah splintered. Ma and Hanumakka came running out of the kitchen. They could not find me on the sofa. They immediately spotted Ajji through the window—she was running towards the lake.

'There was a small bridge which led to a rickety pier on the water. I don't know if it is still there. Ajji had some kind of a demonic strength ... she was nearly half way across the bridge by the time Ma and Hanumakka came running out of the house, screaming.

'Ajji reached the edge of the pier in no time. She smacked my mouth with an open palm. "You had my son throw me out of the house? I'll teach you ... you devil. I'll teach you and your witch of a mother a good lesson." She held me high up, like a throw ball. "I'll throw this piece of filth into the river. I don't care if I die, I'll drag her down with me. Throwing me out of my own son's home." Ajji spat on the ground.

'I screamed and screamed. Ma and Hanumakka were still far off. At least it looked that way to me. I screamed for Alice.

'"I'm here darling, I'm here!" Alice was floating in front of me, her eyes glinting like glass marbles. "Pammi darling, I want you to close your eyes and mouth tightly. The water will feel cold, but Hanumakka will catch you. It is like diving! Remember we did it in summer? Only this time, you won't have the yellow duck balloon around your waist. Okay?"

'"I closed my eyes tightly, but only for a second. I opened them again, to follow Alice's movements. She had glided away from me, and now floated in front of Ajji. I felt Ajji's grasp slacken. I knew. I just knew Ajji was able to see Alice. "Devil! Devil! Devil!" Ajji screamed.

'Ajji still had that pair of scissors tucked into her saree. Alice stared at the scissors and it floated up. "Close your eyes!" Alice screamed, just as I saw the scissors kind of lunge in the air. Ajji's hands slipped away and I was flung into the water.

'I heard another splash just as I hit the water. Hanumakka had dived in immediately. The last I remember of Ajji was seeing her twitching body on the pier ... the pair of scissors sticking out of her neck, glinting in the afternoon sun. There was so much blood. So much. And Ajji's eyes ...'

'That's enough for now, Prerna', I said. Prerna's face glistened with sweat.

'No, doctor, I have to tell you the rest ... '

'No. We will continue tomorrow. You need rest. When I say rest, I don't mean just sleep. You have to disengage your brain.' Hell, I needed to disengage my brain.

'Okay', she said in a small voice.

We sat quietly for a couple of minutes.

'The first few sessions will always be difficult', I said gently. 'Dealing with all these memories is not easy. I want you to do something nice for the rest of the day ... something you enjoy. I have a small library in my office. Why don't I lend you a good book?'

'Actually, if you can give me any mathematics book and some paper, I'd love that.' I must have stared at her in a funny way. She shrugged and said, 'I'm a bit of a nerd. Little bit.'

I could not help but laugh. I downloaded and printed question banks of high school mathematics from the Internet. Prerna appeared delighted when I handed over the printouts.

'If you need me, just dial 1 and ask the reception to page me', I said. I doubt if she even heard me; she was already lost in a world of square-roots and logarithms.

I completed my rounds and caught up on some pending paperwork. Prerna's story had left me exhausted; the prognosis of her case was obviously complex. While narrating the incident,

Prerna had once again become a five-year-old. Her voice had changed; her body language had changed. But more than that, it was unnerving even for me to hear her switch voices—as Alice with a posh British accent and as little Pammi.

I scheduled a separate session with her parents later that afternoon. I had to corroborate Prerna's experience without breaking confidentiality. I understood why they did not want to come back to Nisarga.

'I can never forget that afternoon', Susheela almost whispered. 'Pammi was struggling furiously ... like ... like a goat being led to its slaughter. Those screams ... ' she clapped her ears shut. Rajanna sat straight, staring ahead, dry-eyed.

'I'm sorry that you have to remember all this', I said. 'It's important for me to understand how her case has progressed over the years ... how deeply she has been affected by all this.'

'It all happened very fast, doctor. Hanumakka and I were running towards them. Pammi was squirming ... flopping about ... like a fish caught in a net. That *rakshasi* was getting ready to throw my baby into the water. I think somehow in that moment of struggle, Pammi saw the scissors and ... it was instinct, doctor.'

'By then I also had reached the scene, accompanied by the doctor from H. D. Koté', Rajanna said. 'I mean, we were about to park the jeep when the driver, Nanjunda, yelled and pointed to the pier. We could see my ... the old woman holding up Pammi. Dr Ranga, Nanjunda and myself ... we ran towards the pier. It took us hardly two minutes to reach it, but it was all over. We saw Hanumakka dive into the water. Susheela and I went into shock', Rajanna stopped talking and held his wife's hand tightly.

'It was Dr Ranga who took charge immediately', he continued, his eyes looking at a scene from the past. 'He first attended to Pammi. She had swallowed some water and had to be resuscitated, so he administered CPR. He told Hanumakka and Susheela to take Pammi back to the house. Only after they left, he attended to that woman. We carried her body to the jeep ... that pair of scissors still sticking out of her neck. Dr Ranga instructed Nanjunda to take us to his private clinic instead of the government hospital, to avoid unnecessary attention. He also called the superintendent of police for Koté taluk. I don't know what he managed; how he managed. All I know is he took care of the legal front. I think the superintendent took statements from Hanumakka and Nanjunda. Dr Ranga too was a witness, a very valuable witness, considering he was very well-respected in the area. They decided that the case was so cruel and tragic that it would be very damaging for the child to proceed any further. They ... they decided not to have any paper trail for this case. No FIR was registered. The statements were all oral.

'Dr Ranga removed the scissors and stitched up the wound. Nanjunda, threw the scissors in a well. In the death certificate, Dr Ranga mentioned that the woman died of cardiac arrest. He asked me to call my family and relatives. By the time everyone arrived, her body was ready for last rites, covered in mounds of flowers. So no one really had the chance to see the stitched-up wound. She was cremated in H. D. Koté.'

'How was Pammi after this incident?'

'For about a week, she kept asking about Ajji', Susheela answered, her eyes glistening. 'I think she was so afraid that the old woman will return. But gradually, she got back to her normal self. Her interactions with Alice had increased a lot. We did not worry at that time ... it was helping her to cope, I think. We initially thought of moving back to Bengaluru, but Dr Ranga advised us against it. He pointed out that apart from this gruesome incident, Pammi was a well-adjusted child. Too many changes could destabilise her emotionally. Also, he wanted us to behave normally, so that Pammi wouldn't pick any fear or guilt from us.'

'When did Alice stop visiting?'

'I think when Pammi was 12 or 13. I can't remember. It was a very gradual fading off. Pammi was very good in extracurricular activities, especially sports and drama. So she'd have one practice or the other every evening at school. I guess her mind became occupied with other things and she slowly forgot Alice.'

I nodded. 'Prerna has faced a severe form of abuse. Fear such as this, especially when it takes root in childhood, rarely gets erased from a person's subconscious mind. Despite such a traumatic experience, the fact that she has led a very normal life, positive life I would say, it shows her immense mental strength. My preliminary evaluation is that Alice came into being because Prerna's young mind was unable to cope with the fear and trauma. The mind often finds its own therapeutic cures. As time went by, her mental state became stronger. Her mind no longer needed this Alice crutch. But now, I think something has triggered her fear, because of which Alice is back. The trigger could be something very overt, or it could be a subconscious stress that's been building up.'

'But ... she usually shares everything with us', Rajanna said. 'Even about her relationships.'

I nodded. 'No, it's not something mundane that has triggered this. Definitely not work stress or relationship problems. I will be doing some scans on her—just to rule out any brain abnormalities. I will also bring in Dr Sakshi Gupta. She is a very senior psychiatrist and she specialises in cognitive behavioural therapy. She is the best. I think Prerna will have to remain here for a couple of weeks at least.'

'Yes, absolutely. Whatever it takes.'

It was time for my evening rounds and I took leave of Prerna's parents, promising to give them updates once the tests were done. After my rounds, I called Dr Sakshi who was in New Delhi for a conference. I apprised her of the case, and she agreed to my initial evaluation.

I ran Prerna's case against DSM-5 checklist for schizophrenia, but she did not tick all the boxes. For one, she spoke very cogently and her self-awareness was high. Her interest in mathematics proved her logical functioning was strong. Her imaginary friend had not turned up at the hospital, yet.

The next day, I did a couple of fMRI scans on her. The scans did not reveal any abnormalities in her brain structure. No shrinkage of volume or lesions. I did notice a slightly higher activation of the right parahippocampal gyrus. I researched late into the night on this kind of activation—I was surprised to see the search hits were all from the realm of parapsychology. The research results supported a hypothesis that people who displayed ESP and telekinesis had a similar pattern of activation. Maybe it also resulted in lucid hallucinations, I thought, as I put up the question on the Critical Psychiatric Network. Anyway, Prerna had displayed remarkable stability so far. Her BP was slightly elevated, but other than that, I'd not observed any alarming behavioural changes in her. I was wary of starting her on any kind of drugs without arriving at a confirmed diagnosis.

'Your MRI scans did not reveal anything abnormal', I informed Prerna the next morning as I set up the video recorder for our second session. 'I want to run some blood and urine work too. We can do that tomorrow. Meanwhile, I'll introduce you to a senior expert who will discuss cognitive behavioural therapy with you.'

'*Abba*! What big words! Why do you need my pee though?' she asked.

'I want to investigate any imbalance in your neurotransmitter levels', I said, as seriously as possible. 'That will help me decide on your medication, if required.'

'You enjoy your work a lot, isn't it?' she asked.

'Yes. What about you? Do you enjoy your work?'

'Yes. Very much.'

'Does it get very stressful? Your work?'

She shrugged. 'A normal amount. Good kind of stress.'

'How are your social relationships? Anything special?'

Prerna sighed and gave a sly smile. 'No, doctor. I'm currently single.'

'Have you been in any long-term relationship?'

'Yes. Two. One was in college. We were classmates. We were together for four years. But he went abroad for his higher studies and we ... kind of ... drifted apart. The second one lasted for two years. He got married last year.'

'Want to talk about that?'

'Like ... what?'

'The breakup. How did it affect you?'

'The second one hurt, obviously. Not hurt. More like anger. I mean there was no pressure from my side; I'm not for jumping into matrimony the minute I feel strongly about a guy. I like to get my bearings in a relationship before I can even think of the long haul. But he was under tremendous pressure to go with his parents' choice. I don't think he'd even spoken about me at home. I actually felt sorry for him—who better than me to understand the fear of an elder, yes? Then he told me if only I had long hair and looked like a normal Indian girl, he could have somehow convinced his parents. That's when I dumped his sorry ass.'

'Are you in touch with these two men?'

'Boyfriend number 1, yes. Number 2, no. I don't suffer fools. Anyway, can I tell the rest of my story?'

'Yes, sure. Only if you are up to it.'

'Yes, of course. So things got back to a normal routine after Ajji died. But my bedwetting had become a problem—I peed in my bed almost every night and was terribly ashamed of it. I was afraid of making friends—what if they came to know about my shameful secret? So it was always Alice for me.

'It was nice to have an invisible best friend. I suppose it was also creepy to see me have intense conversations with the air. My parents hoped turning ten would magically put a stop to these problems. So they made a big deal of my tenth birthday. An important milestone had been reached.

'I still remember, doctor. The birthday cake was a chocolate teddy bear with Gems chocolate buttons for eyes, a strawberry for the nose and walnuts for paws. Ten candles flickered and danced on the teddy's tummy. The whole garden was lit up with twinkling lights and balloons. My classmates had come with their parents. So much excitement—no one had ever cut a teddy bear cake.

'I was in a new, shiny white frock—a frilly one with blue lace trimmings that scratched my legs. It was time to cut the cake. Everyone sang Happy Birthday and I blew the candles to much clapping and laughing. Ma cut the cake and fed me a piece. I gave a piece each to Papa and Ma.

'"My turn! My turn!" Alice jumped up and down, clapping her hands.

'I thrust my hand out with a piece of cake. I saw Alice eat it, and we both laughed when the cream made a moustache under her nose. I did not notice that the crowd had gone silent. It must have been quite a scene—me feeding cake to the air and talking to myself. The birthday party wound up pretty quickly after that.

'Word got around real fast in school. The principal called my parents and asked them to take me to a school-recommended child psychologist in Mysore. That fellow used terms like separation anxiety and internalisation of stress. He said I had an invisible friend because I was not getting enough attention from my parents on account of their full-time careers. The bed-wetting was sure proof of that apparently. I don't think my parents told him anything about Ajji's death. Can I have a cup of coffee, doctor?'

I was so immersed in Prerna's story that I was caught off-guard. 'Of course. Why don't you take a break? I'll get the coffee from the cafeteria.'

A couple of minutes later, I was back with the coffee. Prerna blew into the foam and said, 'How I hated him, doctor. I mean that psychologist. He had the oiliest face I've ever come across. His cheeks were pockmarked and it looked like oil pooled in those cavernous pores. His nose and forehead glistened all the time and his spectacles always slid to the edge of his nose. His hair stank of stale coconut oil. It was slicked backwards, making his forehead as wide as his desk. What a refreshing contrast you are, doctor!'

'Why, thank you', I smiled.

Prerna chuckled. 'Anyway, I decided not to talk to him. At all. In one of the sessions, he asked, "Is your friend here with us now? If you don't answer, we'll have to put you in the hospital." I shook my head and cried. Alice was of course there—she was sitting right next to me, making faces at him.

'The sessions went nowhere. Finally, Ma quit her job. I blamed myself. I was proud of Ma and her big office. I thought, maybe if I stopped peeing in bed and stopped talking to Alice when Ma was around, she'd get back to work. She'd think I was cured and I wouldn't have to see that slimy psychologist too. So I stopped sleeping. I'd lie awake all night whispering to Alice. But I'd fall asleep during the day in school and my grades plunged.

'One night, as I lay in bed, Ma and Papa came to my room. Ma's eyes were puffy with tears. She cried a lot these days and it broke my heart. Papa kissed me on my forehead and sat next to me.

'"Darling," Ma whispered, her eyes filling up again. "How can we help you? Tell us."

'In a minute, I was bawling too. In between sobs I said, "Go to office, Ma. I won't pee in the bed, I promise. I will do well in school. Please, Ma. Go to office."

Alice cried with me as Ma and Papa hugged me. Somehow after that night, things fell in place. Ma got a job in my school as an economics teacher. My bed-wetting stopped gradually. Before long, I was scoring good grades and life became busy. I saw less and less of Alice, and by the time I reached my thirteenth birthday, we moved back to Bengaluru and I stopped seeing her altogether.'

'Did you miss her? When you stopped seeing her?'

Prerna thought for a minute. 'It's hard to say. It was all so gradual. It was as natural as losing touch with a school friend when you move homes.'

'What happened next?'

Prerna shrugged. 'Like I said, life was normal. Funnily enough, I never thought about Alice all these years. So imagine my shock when she came back. Seventeen years later, on a Tuesday afternoon. In my office cubicle.

'It was almost three and I was working frantically on a piece of critical code. It had to go live in an hour. I was nearly done and asked my team lead, Ashish, to do a quick code review. Ashish pulled up a chair next to me and began the review. Meanwhile, I had to update some project documentation. That was when the knocking on the window started. I was startled. We were on the seventh floor, and barring the window cleaners, no one could access the windows from outside. The knocking was intermittent and of course, no one was hanging on the window.

'Ashish found a bug in one of the functions and was saying something when the window panes rattled. I jumped. "Did you hear that?" I asked as I turned to the window.

'To my horror, Alice had slid the window open and was struggling to get inside. She finally plopped on the floor.

'"What? What is it?" Ashish asked as he stared at me and the window. I wonder if I told you before, doctor. There was always a faint fragrance of lavender about Alice. It was not a spray perfume … it was more of … you know, the perfume from sachets that you keep in your cupboard and beneath your pillows. This time, all I could get was the dank smell of stagnant water. It was overpowering in my cubicle.

'"At last! I found you!" Alice cheered happily. Her feet were bare and caked with mud. Her nails were dirty and her skin had a bluish tinge. She was still a ten-year-old. Half her face was gone. I could see the skull beneath her eyes.

'I dug into Ashish's arm and screamed. That's the last thing I remember of that episode. I saw Alice again in my home. Only once. This time her face was okay, but she was crying. When she held my hand, I could feel the coldness enter my bones ... ' Prerna hugged herself and rocked to and fro.

'We can stop, Prerna', I said, standing up to turn off the video camera.

Prerna shook her head. 'That poor child. My helpless friend. She did not talk ... that was the only time I saw her cry. It broke my heart, doctor. I mean, she was there for me—in the worst possible time of my life, she was my guardian angel. And now ... she is in some kind of distress ... and it tears me up not knowing what to do. I just took a wild shot, that by coming here, something will happen. That I can help her in some way. But she has not come to me ... I don't know what to do.'

Seeing Prerna cry affected me deeply, and I was taken by surprise by the way I felt. Dangerous territory. 'Prerna, can you think of any reason why Alice came back to you? Last time she came to you because you were in distress. Were you in a similar situation this time?'

Prerna looked up at me, tears still lining her lashes. 'No ... this time she came to me because she is in distress. I know ... I know how all this sounds. Ashish could not see her; no one can see her. The rational part of my mind says Alice is a hallucination. But ... but I know, doctor. There is something more to it. I just know it.' Her breathing had become shallow, and her fists were balled.

'Okay, let's try something here', I said in a low tone. I had to get her attention. 'The camera is not running, so this is unofficial, between you and me.'

She wiped her face on the sleeve of her gown and looked at me questioningly.

'There are really two decision paths we can work on. The first is based on the assumption that Alice is a hallucination. The second is based on the assumption that Alice is real, okay?' I drew a flowchart on a sheet of paper and showed it to her. Her face brightened—logic was her territory.

'Go on', she said.

'So let's say, Alice is a hallucination. She came to you when you were most distressed as a child. Your mind needed a support to maintain a balance. You were already enamoured by Alice and all her adventures. So your mind projected Alice. You got better, your mind became stronger, Alice faded away. So going by this theory, something must have affected your mind again for Alice to have come back. Some trigger. Can you think of anything out of ordinary you have done in the past six months?'

Prerna shrugged. 'I enrolled for a meditation course. I'm not the type at all. But I enrolled anyway. I thought it was a passing fad, but I quite love it. It has become a part of my routine.'

'Anything else?'

Prerna shook her head.

'Okay. So let us look at the second assumption. If Alice is real, then we must find out more about the Halliday family. So both of us have some homework to do, okay?' I gave her a small ruled notebook. 'You write down whatever you've done in the last six months. Whatever comes to your mind. It could be something as simple as a meal you ate to an argument you had. Okay?'

She nodded like a child. 'And what is your homework?'

'I will find out about Alice.'

I left her in buoyed spirits. But I was worried. The latest Alice hallucination had pretty strong olfactory and auditory components. I wondered if it was the commencement of a downward spiral. Every time I watched her videos, and heard two voices coming out of her mouth, I felt a chill. I feared that there could be time intervals when Prerna regressed to a place in her childhood, got stuck there like a scratchy cassette. She was probably not even aware of the lapsed time.

I worked late into the night on her case. I made copious notes from her video and made a list of journals I wanted to refer to. I must've fallen asleep on my desk. I felt a cold palm on my neck and heard a whisper that simply said, 'Pammi!' I woke up startled, sensing the faint aroma of lavender. I almost screamed when the phone on my desk rang. It was Nagraj. 'You have to come immediately to see this. It is the Bengaluru patient.'

I ran to the reception where Nagraj sat behind an array of screens. He tapped on one of the screens showing the CCTV feed from Prerna's room. Prerna was sitting up on her bed, clearly talking to someone. Then she held out her arms as if beckoning the person into an embrace. Next, she hugged the air and kissed repeatedly. She then acted as if she was tucking this someone into bed. She kissed the pillow some more and fell asleep.

'I've seen all kinds of things. But this made my hair stand up', Nagraj said, extending his arm in evidence. 'You look like shit, doctor. Why don't you get some sleep? If there is any further movement here, I will page you.'

I shook my head. 'I will wait for an hour or so to make sure she is okay.'

I eventually returned to my cottage and fell into an exhausted, disturbed sleep. I dreamt that Alice watched me as I slept. I dreamt of Prerna, and there was nothing remotely doctor–patient about it. I was glad when the night ended and I woke up in cold sweat, just around sunrise, with a decision ringing in my head. I could no longer continue as Prerna's doctor. I was too affected by her, and her case. The power of suggestion is an intense mind-bending tool—no wonder I'd felt Alice's presence last evening. Sure, I could pin that down to stress, a weak moment. But I had another disturbing realization. I was attracted to Prerna. Very strongly.

Without thinking, I called Dr Sakshi who was scheduled to return to Nisarga that day. It was only when the call connected that I realised it was just half-past-five in the morning. I was about to hang up when Dr Sakshi answered.

'Sri? So early in the morning?'

'This case I've been discussing with you ... I mean I'm sorry for calling you at this hour. Shall I call back?'

'No ... it's perfectly fine. You are talking about Prerna Rajanna?'

'Yes. I would like to transfer the case over to you. I ... I don't think I can deal with it objectively any longer.'

'I will talk to Girija and fit Prerna's appointments in my schedule. What is troubling you?'

'I want a personal counselling session.'

'I'll put that as high priority. Meet me at one this afternoon. We can meet Prerna after your session.'

'Yes, sure.' My voice waivered.

'Sri, are you okay?'

'Yes ... I'm just stressed, I guess.'

'Okay. I'll see you later then?'

I freshened up, put on my trainers and was off for a pounding run. If not anything, the physical activity would dissipate the confusion and depression that clung to me. By the end of the eighth kilometre, I had a plan to find out about Alice.

The Hallidays had to go to church somewhere. Assuming Alice was born here, she'd have been baptised. There'd be some records of that. Using those documents, I could get in touch with one of those ancestry investigating firms in UK ... assuming the Hallidays had moved back to their country. It was all a very long shot; at least, I could honestly tell Pammi that I had tried my best. Perhaps knowing more about Alice and her family would help Pammi in some way.

Only one church came to my mind—St Philomena's in Mysore, one of the oldest and most important churches of the district. The timeline fit in well too—the foundation stone was laid in 1933, commissioned by the Wodeyars. Pammi said the Hallidays seemed to socialise with the Mysore royalty. I could almost imagine all of them attending the first prayer service in St Philomena's in 1941. I looked at my watch. It was nearing seven. I took a quick shower and started for Mysore.

I reached the church a little after eight. There was a modest gathering for the morning mass. It had been quite a while since I'd stepped inside a place of worship, and I fidgeted uneasily now. After the mass, I unobtrusively approached one of the church staff and said, rather foolishly, 'Excuse me, I would like to talk to someone. Like a priest.'

'You mean for a confession?' The young man asked.

'No. I wanted to know about ... about some family members who were a part of this church in the 1940s.'

'Oh, like that. I'm not sure. You will have to talk to the cathedral's parish priest—Father William. But he is travelling today. But you do one thing ... you can talk to Father Thomas. He's been here forever. Come I'll take you to him.'

Father Thomas was ambling about in the church courtyard, enjoying the sunshine, a rosary constantly twitching between his thumb and forefinger. 'Father Thomas is the youngest of us all', my guide said with a mischievous smile. 'Ninety-six years young. Wily as a fox.'

I smiled and looked at the shrivelled old man, slightly hunched. We approached him and my guide said, 'Father Thomas, someone is here to see you.'

Age had withered the face, but had left the piercing eyes unscathed. 'Very well, boy. Go back to your work now.' There was a slight tremor in the voice, but I guessed it had been a rousing choir voice in its heyday. My guide left. Father Thomas stared at me unabashedly for a few moments. 'Stand in the sun. I want to see your face clearly.'

I changed my position and stood sheepishly as directed.

'Hmm. Walk with me. There ... to that bench where the sun shines', he pointed with his walking stick. 'You are not a believer. Yet you seek.'

I smiled.

After we were seated, I said, 'Yes, Father. I'm looking for some information.'

Father Thomas laughed. 'All your answers are in there', he pointed to the church, 'and yet you ask me, an old man waiting impatiently for death, for information?'

I smiled. 'It's not what you think—'

'Do you believe in god? Humour me', he said, and added in a conspiratorial tone, 'sometimes I find it difficult too.'

I had to laugh. 'I'm agnostic.'

'What do you do for a living? I know ... I know ... it is a weekday and a young man like you must be running to work at this time. Yet, you are here, sitting next to an old man looking for information. It must be important. If you are getting impatient, tell me. It's just that I don't get much company that I enjoy. They are all very boring', he said shaking his stick in the direction of the church.

'I'm a psychiatrist, Father.'

'Oh! So you study one of the greatest creations of our Lord. Good. Good. But what is a psychiatrist doing in a church?'

'I am looking for information on Lord James Halliday. He lived around these parts in the 1940s—'

'And died on August 15, 1947', Father Thomas finished.

'Died?'

Father Thomas nodded. 'I was twenty-six or twenty-seven then. I was already with this church. Lord Halliday was a wonderful man. What is your name, doctor?'

'Srinidhi.'

'He was a generous man, Srinidhi. Very generous. He made significant contributions towards education in the local area. Donated a lot of money towards agriculture and irrigation projects too. He married an Indian lady. You know, when their child was born, they had a prayer service in Chamundi temple first. The church was still being built, so the child's baptism was delayed. I can't remember if it took place eventually.'

'What happened to them?'

'Ah. India became independent. Lord Halliday arranged for a big celebration in the entire district. Someone asked him if he is so happy because he can go back to his country. He looked at them squarely in the eye and said, "This is my home." August 15 was also their child's birthday. She had turned ten. As a gift, Lord Halliday had commissioned the building of a boat ... it came all the way from his country.

'The family inaugurated the boat by sailing down the Kabini. Everything went on well. They returned to their home by evening I think. You know they lived near Kakanakote by a huge lake. No one knows what happened. The next day, the bodies of Lord and Lady Halliday were found floating on the lake. The boat and the child were gone.'

'Gone in the sense?' The sunshine no longer felt warm.

'I think they went boating in the lake. They must have met with an accident. I don't know. A lot of people tried to look for the little girl. That lake is very deep. Very deep. Have you seen how still its surface is? It is fed by Kabini. For nearly a week, people kept taking turns in diving. But those days, where did we have advanced underwater kits? Some of the divers said they spotted what looked like the boat, but they were not sure. But almost everyone said there was a current under the surface—even whirlpools—suggesting the lake is draining back to the river through some narrow opening. After ten days, it was clear that the child won't be found. We buried the Hallidays there only, on the banks of the lake. At least that way, they could protect their child.'

We sat in silence for some time.

'But why are you asking about them?' Father Thomas asked.

'Oh ... I work in Nisarga Psychiatric Research Centre. The

Hallidays' bungalow is a part of the hospital. I ... I just found some old photos ... I was curious.'

Father Thomas was staring at my face as I gave my explanation. I could not meet his eye. I thanked him and took his leave. As I started for the car park, Father Thomas called out, 'Son, help her.'

I looked at him questioningly.

'Alice. I know the child has come back. Help her. Don't be afraid.'

I stood still for a moment, my heart juddering. I wanted to ask the Father how he knew but figured it was futile. I was sure I wouldn't get a rational explanation. As I returned his piercing stare, I understood he just knew. It was one of those unexplainable facts of existence where one becomes cognizant of certain realities at a very deep level, bypassing inputs from the physical senses and logical reasoning.

I reached Nisarga around noon. I had a quick lunch and although I wanted to see Pammi, I restrained myself and prepared for my session with Dr Sakshi.

'I have looked at the video transcripts', Dr Sakshi said as we settled down for my session. Two years away from retirement, she was the senior-most doctor of the hospital. Not to mention one of the best in her field. 'But I want to listen to what you think about the case.'

I gave her all the details of the case and my analysis. I also told her about my latest discussion with Pammi and that I'd been to St Philomena's to find out more about Alice.

Dr Sakshi got up and walked to the coffee machine in her office. 'You want a cup, Sri? You look like you could use many.'

I nodded.

'Your finding about the higher activation of right parahippocampal gyrus is very interesting. Did you get a response from the Psychiatry Network?'

'I've not yet checked, doctor.'

'Your hypothesis that the unusual activation pattern in her brain could have led to the lucid hallucinations sounds very plausible', Dr Sakshi said, handing over the coffee. She pulled out some stapled sheets from a mountain of files on her desk. 'I was looking up research papers. See this. The cortical mass changes as the brain develops through childhood and adolescence. It is possible that given the trauma, and the inherent activation pattern in her brain, she was projecting Alice. Now, this stopped in her thirteenth year. She was stepping into adolescence; a lot of changes take place inside her body. It is possible that the activation pattern changed, and she was no longer able to see Alice. Also, the environmental factors changed in her favour too. Now, look at this paper', Dr Sakshi pushed another set of stapled sheets towards me. 'This research gives a remarkable example of brain plasticity. Constant practise of meditation increases cortical thickness. Prerna mentioned that she practises meditation regularly. It is possible that meditation has somehow activated the regions that enable such vivid hallucinations.'

'Yes ... ' I said unsurely.

'Of course, the case looks more complicated. I saw how she regressed to her childhood, speaking in the tone of a five-year-old when she narrated those incidents. And how smoothly she switches to what she imagines to be Alice's voice.'

'Yes, it seems to me her mind is so fragile, just tottering on a seesaw.'

'I am looking up some case studies ... just to study the prognosis of dissociative personality disorder. But you know ... we both could be really wrong.'

'I know ... we are clutching at straws in a hurricane here.'

'I mean, for all you know, it may not be a hallucination at all.'

I looked at Dr Sakshi in surprise.

'Sounds daft, isn't it? But I think, while we should absolutely work within the framework offered by science, we should also keep our minds open to all possibilities. It is not about us, but about Prerna. We have to do what is best for her. So here is what I suggest. Don't tell her about how Alice and her parents died. Tell her that you found out from the church records that the Hallidays moved back to England. Let's see if that news has a placebo effect. I also intend to ease her off meditation for a while—if it's causing the additional stimulation, then the hallucinations should stop.'

'Okay.'

'Meanwhile ... ' Dr Sakshi stared into her cup, a frown creasing her brow. 'In the off-chance that this is not a hallucination,

I suggest you go ahead with your line of investigation. Find the Halliday's resting place and little Alice, if it's possible at all. Of course, this is unofficial. You are going to do this on your own time, as a personal quest. If anyone asks, we never discussed this.'

I gave a short laugh. Dr Sakshi was the best not because of her technical expertise but because she never shut the door on any possibility.

'It's been what ... five years since you came here?' she asked me in a softer, non-doctor tone.

'Yeah.'

'Hmm. For five years, you've had no social life. You've lived like a monk. So, along comes this girl. She's smart, sassy and damaged. You find yourself attracted to her. You develop a strong emotional bond. There is nothing wrong with that, doctor. You have identified your feelings and have done what is right, professionally. I don't want you to feel guilty. A good psychiatrist does not necessarily have to be a cold bastard.'

Our session with Pammi went well. She seemed quite comfortable with Dr Sakshi and bought our explanation that she only needed behavioural therapy. She listened with interest about my visit to St Philomena's church. I told her about Father Thomas and that the Hallidays had returned to England after India won her independence. She thanked me over and over again for all my efforts. It did look like the news had found its mark and Pammi would be on the mend soon.

At the end of the session, Dr Sakshi wanted to stay on for a couple of minutes to talk to Pammi about cognitive behavioural therapy. I excused myself and got up. I'd just reached the door when a voice stopped me. 'Doctor?' I felt a cold shaft run up my spine, numbing me. The voice was neither Pammi's nor Dr Sakshi's. It was Pammi's version of Alice's voice. I turned around slowly.

Dr Sakshi was staring at Pammi's face intently; there was something different about it. Subtle changes like the lift in the corner of her lips and the narrowing of her eyes.

'Did you ever wonder how Pammi got your direct number?' I saw Pammi's lips move as 'Alice' asked the question.

I did not reply.

'I told her, doctor. I often sit next to you when you watch the deer ... '

My intestines felt woozy as I watched Pammi's face slacken. She fell back gently on the pillows and seemed fast asleep. I had never given that first telephone call a thought. My line was unlisted and only hospital staff knew the number. But that did not bother me. Not as much as the detail about Alice sitting next to me as I watched the deer. I had never mentioned the deer to Pammi. Not once.

I jumped as Dr Sakshi touched my elbow. 'What was all that about?'

'Dr Sakshi, keep her under observation. I have some urgent work to do.' I did not wait for Dr Sakshi to ask any more questions; I was running down the stairs two at a time.

'Nagraj!' I called out as I ran towards the door. 'Come with me. Now.'

In a second, Nagraj and I were jogging side by side. 'Get two or three of those construction workers and meet me by the lake. Ask them to come with shovels.' Nisarga was expanding one of the wings, so we always had construction workers on the site.

I usually sat on a rocky outcropping to watch the deer. It was on an elevated piece of land overlooking the lake. I'd not been to the place for over a week. When Nagraj came back with four young men, all armed with shovels and picks, I led them towards the spot.

The earth beneath the rock had caved in because of heavy downpours over the past few days. I stepped on the loose soil gingerly and slipped a good two feet downwards. Only the sturdy root of a dangerously bent tree prevented my freefall into the lake. The men yelled as I slipped. One of them handed me a shovel, and using that as a support, I hauled myself up and clambered over the rock. I asked the men to find a way to get to the rock.

We began scraping soil and vegetation off the rock's surface. Even before we had cleaned half-way, I felt as if I'd stuck electrodes on my raw heart. This was no rock at all—it was a gravestone. Rather, two grave stones resting side by side. I could see the word 'Lord' on one of them.

It would take just another downpour for the soil to cave in completely. Whatever remained beneath the grave stones would wash down to the lake too. I could imagine the wooden coffins, rotting by now, smashed to smithereens under the weight of a mound of loose soil, and the bones of Alice's parents lying scattered on the lake bed. Is this the reason why Alice came back? To save the last cord of bond she had with the remnants of her parents?

'This is the grave of the original owners of this place', I said to no one in particular. The men stopped their scraping and looked at me. 'I will get permission to have their remains moved to a better place. But this won't survive for long. Can you build a temporary support to hold the soil?' I looked at each of the men.

'Yes, saar', one of them answered after crossing his heart. 'We can insert some bamboo sticks and build a temporary support.' He stamped the soil and watched lumps of it fall away into the lake. 'But the support will hold only for a few days.'

'I will get things moving fast', I said. 'Nagraj, will you oversee this?'

'Yes, you don't worry.' My respect for Nagraj shot up tremendously. I could see so many questions on his face, yet, he held back. He just trusted me that this was urgent and important; the questions could come later. I think it was just a glance between us—we both knew our friendship had become stronger.

Dr Sakshi, when she believes in a person's motives, can get men to move Everest. Like Nagraj, she asked no questions, but got down to making calls. By next morning, the legal team was working with the local magistrate to exhume the graves and shift the remains to a 'site respectable of the owners of Nisarga land', according to an official email I received.

We did not reveal the new development to Pammi. Personally, I was convinced Alice was no hallucination; there was something more going on, something my rational mind did not understand.

Over the next two days, the legal formalities were completed and the graves were exhumed. The remains of Lord and Lady Halliday were interred in brand new coffins in the presence of a priest from St Mary's church in H. D. Koté, police and a magistrate. Nagraj had worked with Basappa, our gardener, to prepare the new burial site within the compound walls of Nisarga. It was lush with well-tended rose shrubs and bougainvillea. In a sombre, yet touching ceremony, Lord and Lady Halliday were once again laid to rest below the earth. They were given new headstones, and I was overwhelmed to see that all the staff and construction workers took turns in visiting the graves and showering flowers.

In these two days, Alice had not visited Pammi. I felt at peace, although my heart ached for little Alice. She should have been here with her parents, I thought. That night as I turned in, she came in my dream. I found myself in Pammi's room in the dream. I was standing behind her bed, watching Alice. Alice sat at the foot of Pammi's bed, chatting with her. I could not hear what they spoke; it was just two little girls gibbering away. I heard Pammi's high-pitched voice, interspersed with Alice's more controlled and modulated tones. Then, Alice produced a pair of scissors.

'It's the hair, Pammi. If not for my long hair, I could have been with Mum and Dad.'

'Here, let me help you, you poor darling', Pammi said and moved closer to Alice. I heard the crunch of the steel blades on the brittle hair, and I saw Alice's long locks floating to the floor.

'Will you be with me, Pammi? Please darling. When you went away, and Mum and Dad kept slipping in the soil, I was so, so alone. It's so cold and dark down there', Alice began to weep.

Pammi held her, stroked her hair and kissed her repeatedly on the forehead. 'Of course, I will never leave you alone ... we are best friends forever, remember? You poor dear.'

'Come, let's go', Alice said, holding Pammi's hand. Pammi stood up happily. The two of them turned to me. Pammi with a vacant smile, Alice, now only a skull with tufts of hair.

'Bye-bye, Doctor', they chorused, turned around and went skipping away as if they were playing hopscotch.

I woke up to the incessant banging on my door. I was drenched in sweat that stank of my fear.

'Sri! Wake up!'

I was surprised to hear Dr Sakshi's voice. It was about Pammi. I just knew it. I flew to the door.

'Pammi is not in her room ... she ... '

'We have to get to the lake', I said as I pulled on a pair of shoes, unmindful of the fact that I was clad in a vest and boxers.

'No, we spotted her walking towards the gravesite. Nagraj is following her ... she seems to be sleepwalking.'

We walked briskly towards the grave. Sure enough, in the halogen streetlight masked by the fog, I saw the tiny figure of Pammi in the hospital gown trudging up. Her right hand was extended and swinging, as if she were holding someone's hand.

Pammi approached the grave and stood there for a couple of minutes. She kept nodding her head and whispering something to the air next to her. Then she turned around and started retracing her steps.

We figured she'd head back to her room. But she stopped midway and looked up at the ten feet high compound wall. She seemed to discuss something with her companion. She walked towards the wall and patted it, as if feeling for a support. In a second, she was scaling the smooth facade like a lizard.

It was Dr Sakshi's shriek that broke my trance. There was no way I could climb the wall. I had to run all the way to the exit to get to the other side—a good three minutes—by which time Pammi had disappeared. I heard footsteps pounding behind me—it was Nagraj.

'To the lake', I yelled. There was no time to run on the paved path to reach the bank. I plunged into a thickly wooded slope, branches whipping me and tearing at my flesh. I reached the bank of the lake, only to find Pammi many yards ahead. She was already wading in the water.

'Pammi!' I screamed as I ran towards her, hopping as I took my shoes off. I was still far off when her head disappeared under water. I dived.

The lake felt like a million shards of glass piercing my overheated body. I swam at a pace where I thought my arms would disengage from my body. But I reached her. I saw ripples on the opposite side, and I figured Nagraj had reached her too. We pulled her up, but she wouldn't come. She struggled against us, balled herself up and kicked Nagraj in the chest. He immediately slackened his grip and hugged himself.

'Nagraj!' I screamed. 'Don't let her go!'

By then I saw a couple of more men dive into the lake and swim towards us. I was losing my grip on Pammi; something powerful was dragging her downwards. Father Thomas had mentioned whirlpools and I yelled for the men to swim faster.

But Pammi went underwater completely, dragging me along. I heard a voice in my head, angry and sobbing, 'Let her go! We want to be together!' I saw a pair of hands clamped on Pammi's feet, tugging her.

'Alice, honey, if Pammi goes with you, her parents will be very sad—like your Mum and Dad', I replied in my mind. 'Let Pammi go and I promise I will come back for you. I will take you back to your Mum and Dad.'

The tugging slowed down, but I could still see the hands on Pammi's ankles. Something broke inside me. 'If I can't find you, darling, then I'll ... I'll stay with you. Let Pammi go. Please, baby. Let Pammi go.'

I saw her then. Alice. Her face so angelic, so afraid and lonely. She let go. The men pulled us out of the water. Pammi was administered CPR by Dr Sakshi. I lay on the clayey bank, coughing, tears streaming down for a reason I could not fathom.

'My cottage is the nearest. Help me take her there', I heard Dr Sakshi tell the men who'd dragged us out of the water. 'Sri, can you walk?'

I nodded. I saw Nagraj sitting cross-legged a distance away, panting. He got up and held out a hand to pull me up. 'Better to get out of wet clothes soon. This fog is not good', he said. I stood up unsteadily. My legs buckled and I flopped to a kneeling position. 'Give me a minute', I rasped. It had to be me ... I had to carry Pammi back to the cottage. She was so waif-like; I could haul her on my shoulders in a fireman's lift quite easily. Surely my legs had that much strength?

But thank god for Dr Sakshi's presence of mind—she had two men wheel a gurney all the way down to the lake. Pammi was placed on it and wheeled to Dr Sakshi's cottage. Nurses were summoned and Pammi was left in their adept care. Pammi seemed to be fast asleep.

Dr Sakshi passed around dry towels and cups of hot tea. Soon, everyone left, except Nagraj and me.

'Go and get some sleep ... both of you', Dr Sakshi said.

I nodded. 'She's down there. Alice. I saw her. Communicated with her.'

Dr Sakshi did not say anything.

I saw Nagraj nodding next to me, fear stretching his face. 'I don't know who you are talking about ... but I saw something.'

'Check Prerna's ankles, doctor', I said before leaving.

I slept well into the afternoon the next day. By evening, I was physically refreshed, but a mental lethargy blanketed me. I sat on my porch, looking at the sunset over the lake. The goddamn, murderous lake. I was sick of it all. The forest, the deer, the bleeding sun, the molten water, the hospital, my career, my life—yes, I was sick of it all. I was so caught up in my dark thoughts that I did not notice Dr Sakshi till she pulled a chair next to me.

'I always envied the view you have from your cottage', Dr Sakshi said.

I did not reply.

'I had a long session with Prerna's parents this morning. Brought them up to speed on all that's been happening. They were understandably upset.'

'I don't know what to do. I feel so helpless, Dr Sakshi', I whispered.

'I saw the marks on Prerna's ankles. Gripped by a tiny pair of hands, going by measurements. Tomorrow, a salvage boat is being brought here to the lake. A sophisticated one with SONAR. The one they use for oceanographic studies.'

I turned to look at Dr Sakshi.

'You can go on that. And find Alice.'

The discovery of Lord and Lady Halliday's graves had caused quite a buzz in the local media apparently. They applauded Nisarga for its sensitivity. So when Dr Sakshi wrote to the management saying she believed, on very credible authority, that a little girl was still on the lakebed and deserved to be reunited with her parents, it was taken at highest priority. The salvage operation was arranged. A local TV channel got exclusive filming rights.

'You are a remarkable woman, Dr Sakshi', I said.

She smiled and got up to leave. 'Better shave for tomorrow. You'll be on TV.'

The boat arrived by noon the next day. It was an impressive salvage tugboat, often used for marine salvage. They'd transported it on a massive eighteen-wheeler truck from Mangalore port. The truck could only manoeuvre to the narrowest bank of the lake. After much discussion, it was decided that a temporary harbour had to be built to launch the vessel.

The crew discussed a design with Nisarga's construction team. The construction workers were excited—this was new and innovative, refreshingly different from building walls and fitting windows. The rudimentary harbour would take two days, with twenty workers working round the clock. Alice had to wait.

On the day of the vessel launch, people from nearby towns and villages lined the banks of the lake. The crane on the truck gently lowered the tugboat onto a flat platform with wheels, parked on the sloping harbour. The platform was controlled by a hydraulic system that could move it forward towards the water. Once the vessel had reached the depth to float, the platform could be disengaged and retracted.

Many people came up to the tugboat, touched its hull and touched their eyes as if the vessel was something holy. Some women came with aarti paraphernalia and did puja to the boat. 'Find the little girl', they prayed to it.

Despite the grim aim of the operation, the atmosphere was almost festive. The TV crew panned the camera on the crowd and spoke to a couple of excited onlookers. They wanted to interview me; I let them talk to Nagraj instead. He had worn a crisp blue shirt and a new pair of jeans for the occasion. I slipped away quietly and got on board the boat. I was welcomed warmly by the crew, who'd become good friends over these last couple of days.

The priest from the local Ganapati temple consulted his *panchanga* and proclaimed the time of the launch. He did a *mangalarthi* to the boat and the customary coconut was broken on the ground. At precisely 11:10 a.m., much to the roaring cheer of a hundred faces, *Triveni* glided smoothly on the placid surface of the lake.

Within an hour, the SONAR onboard had detected potential wreckage at a depth of about seventy-five feet. A robotic camera was lowered and we crowded around a small computer screen that was receiving real time images from the camera. As the camera went deeper, the images became grainier. For nearly twenty minutes, we saw nothing but the murky water illuminated in a narrow cone of light emitted by the camera. All of a sudden, Alice's face filled the screen and I staggered back with a shout. Everyone turned around to look at me—of course, no one had seen the face.

'I saw something ... perhaps the boat', I stammered, suddenly conscious that the TV camera was rolling.

Velumurugan, the skipper, manipulated the movement of the camera on what looked like a joystick. The camera turned this way and that, and finally, we saw the outline of a boat. Alice was back, mouthing something. I watched her carefully. She said, 'I'm behind the boat.'

The camera was retracted and four men began to suit up.

'Look, please ... please allow me to go', I begged Velu. The crew knew I was the one who'd found the Halliday graves. I wanted to be there when Alice was found.

Velu shook his head. 'I can't. We've discussed this before. Not only will I be endangering your life, I will be putting others at risk too. The wreckage is at seventy-five feet depth. If there are underwater currents, then it can drag you down. The deepest part of this lake is 280 feet. These are professional divers. There's no way I can allow you.'

'It's not like diving into a swimming pool', Velu had told me, when I'd first broached the subject a couple of days ago.

'I have a C-card', I'd shown him my diving certificate. 'I got it when I was a student in London. This is from British Sub-Aqua Club.'

Velu had examined my laminated card politely. 'What's your range?'

'It's only recreational scuba diving. Max 35 metres.'

'That's ... like ... ' Velu punched some numbers on his mobile phone calculator. 'Nearly 112 feet. When was the last time you went deep?'

'Three years ago', I answered softly.

'Sorry, man. I just can't take the risk', Velu had said, handing back my C-card.

I knew Velu was right, and as the skipper, he could order me ashore if I continued to pester him.

I walked up to Ambi, the most experienced diver. He was getting ready for the dive. 'Don't ask me how I know it. The little girl is behind the boat. The forest trees ... their roots are in the lake. I ... I think she's stuck between the roots ... ' Even as I spoke, an image flashed in my head. 'Scissors. You have to carry a pair of scissors. Or a knife. She had long hair', I closed my eyes, as if I could see something, and continued talking. 'Yes, her hair has become knotted in the vegetation. You have to cut it to release her.'

Ambi looked at Velu and something passed between them.

'Okay, doctor. You are behaving as if your own child is down there', Velu said. He pointed to a diving kit. 'Even a small hint of discomfort, you will be brought back up. You will be supervised at all times by Ambi. You have to follow his instructions. Strictly.'

Even before he finished his speech, I stripped down to my underwear and pulled up the diving suit. I wanted to be underwater before he changed his mind.

'What's the decompression plan?' I looked at Ambi as someone strapped the oxygen cylinders on my back.

Ambi smiled as if to say, 'Well done. You have not forgotten your training.' He spread a decompression chart in front of me. 'On our way back, we will do a safety stop at forty feet for two minutes; one minute at thirty feet; two minutes at twenty feet; five minutes at fifteen; two minutes at ten; seven minutes at five feet. You just follow my cue.'

We strapped hooks from two hydraulic levers and went underwater. The hooks would be used to secure the wreckage and the levers would haul it up.

It was only in the dark, liquid silence that I realised how much I missed being underwater. We swam in an arrow formation—one experienced diver in front, followed by Ambi and me, and two other divers behind us. At about seventy-two feet, I had a tingling sensation—I don't know if it was because of nitrogen narcosis or because the torch lights on our helmet had caught the outline of the boat, wedged in a loamy bed reticulated with roots. The bed seemed to be a plateau of sorts, and the surrounding darkness meant it dropped off in a cliff to greater depths. If the boat had missed this plateau, it would've been lost forever.

I had expected to see only the carcass of the boat, so I was surprised by how much of it remained intact. Parts of the hull had rotted away, and the bow was considerably damaged, but overall it was in a reasonably good condition. The four divers got to work quickly, swimming around the boat to determine the best places to fix the hooks.

Where are you, honey? I thought as I swam towards a wall of underwater roots that went into the plateau. Ambi swam next to me with a menacing bolo knife in hand. He hacked the roots effortlessly and made way to manoeuvre our bodies. He pointed to the cylinders and I understood—we did not have much time, and we could not afford to get entangled here.

'Alice', I called out in my head.

I heard a sigh to my left, and I saw a flash of colour, something blue. I pointed in that direction to Ambi and he chopped some more roots. He saw her first and went still. Her skull had been pulled back, as if the roots were yanking her hair. Most of her hair follicles had decayed, and her hair had probably floated away. Tufts that remained attached to her skull were knotted around the roots. But what wrenched my heart was her frock. Blue in colour. Her birthday frock, probably. It was frayed considerably. It was possibly made of polyester or Rayon, so it had not decayed completely, unlike cotton or silk. She was dangling, like a doll fixed to the rear-view mirror of a car.

We swam to her; Ambi chopped off her hair and she floated free into my arms. I was afraid of scattering her bones if I moved too quickly. By then, the four other divers came near us. We managed to move Alice to the boat. Ambi pointed to the deck. We placed Alice on the deck and covered her with a tarpaulin sheet that we'd carried for this operation. Ambi made signs that he'd swim over her, holding her in place.

One of the divers made radio contact with *Triveni* and gave instructions to start the hauling. We coordinated the lift with our decompression stops and finally, we broke surface.

Once aboard, I realised the tarpaulin sheet covering Alice stank of fish. 'Get something better for her', I shouted to no one in particular. Then, I had a scuffle with the TV crew—there was no way I'd allow them to film Alice that way. It was only when Ambi stepped in, with the bolo knife, that the crew piped down. 'We will put the little one respectfully in a coffin. You can film after that', he said, tapping the camera lens with the handle of the knife.

Someone brought a printed handloom bed sheet to cover Alice. 'Is it washed?' I asked, my voice high-pitched.

'It is new', Velu said gently, putting an arm around my shoulder. 'I bought it on a stopover in Mangalore—wanted to take it home.'

I covered Alice and wept like a father who'd lost his only child.

The divers stood around me, offering me privacy in this strange grief. I composed myself after a couple of minutes.

'Come', Ambi said gently. 'See this boat you rescued. I've not come across such superb mahogany.' We walked around the boat. 'See this', he said kneeling in front of the stern. A rusty metal plate was embossed with the lettering 'Built for Lord Halliday'. Below it, in italics, the name 'Bryont, Craft & Sons, Boat Builders, Devon' was etched.

I walked around the boat towards the starboard. A surge of electricity spiked in my spine. A long metal plate had the name of the boat embossed on it—PRERNA. Below it, 'Inspiration for life' was etched. I staggered, unable to grapple with what I was seeing.

It was four in the evening, and there was a lot of activity going on around me. We had to get *Triveni* back to the temporary harbour, and then transport Alice and the Hallidays' boat into Nisarga. We had to arrange a coffin for Alice, give her a proper burial.

We took the remains of Alice to the hospital morgue. The doctors carefully removed the frock and kept it aside. They cleaned her bones deftly as I watched on. My Alice had a couple of broken ribs and splintered hip. I imagined the boat sinking, for whatever reason. It must have gone down pretty fast. I imagined Alice's parents swimming desperately, yelling for Alice. I heard them gulp air and dive down, only for a minute or two before they resurfaced for another gulp. By then, Alice was deep down, broken and splintered. As the boat hit the plateau, Alice's floating hair must have gotten entangled in the roots, lifting her clean off the boat.

The burial took place the next day, at the crack of dawn to avoid the crowds. Dr Sakshi had arranged for Father Thomas to be brought to Nisarga to perform Alice's last rites. Nagraj had taken care of the coffin as well as got the gravesite ready. Dr Sakshi and I decided that Pammi should attend the service. She stood away from all of us, weeping bitterly. Her parents were equally affected and looked on helplessly at their child.

The service was done. After sixty-seven years, Alice was back with her mum and dad. Father Thomas took me aside before leaving and said, 'I often wondered why He is not calling me. Why was I still here? What purpose did He have for me? I think I got my answer today.'

After everyone dispersed, Pammi, her parents and I gathered in Dr Sakshi's cottage.

'I think this has been very emotionally draining for all of us', Dr Sakshi said as she offered coffee and biscuits. 'I can very truthfully say that this is beyond anything I've come across.'

'It was Alice all along', Pammi said quietly. Her eyes were bloodshot and puffy and it felt like a whiplash to see her face pinched with pain. 'It was not a hallucination ... never was. She was always there with me ... she saved my life.'

'You came back for her when she needed you the most', I said softly. 'You did not let her down. It is only because of you that Alice is back with her parents.'

'I'd like you to remain here for a couple more days. Just to make sure ... you know ... ' Rajanna said unsurely, looking at his daughter.

Pammi shook her head. 'No, Papa. Alice is now resting. Finally. She won't come back. I won't see her anymore', Pammi was racked by sobs. 'I ... I can feel her absence ... like ... like a foetus that has bled out of me.'

Her parents comforted her, but it was only Dr Sakshi who managed to calm her down.

'I believe you, my dear. You are now going through extreme grief brought on by bereavement', Dr Sakshi said. 'Stay on for a couple of days and let the grief run its course. Visit Alice every day. If you feel like, you can have a counsellor to help you.'

Pammi stayed on for four more days. I avoided her assiduously. I was afraid ... afraid that my eyes, my words, my face would give the truth away. That I was intensely in love with her. It was unexplainable. I felt connected to Pammi in a way I did not understand. All I knew was that the connection ran deep, very deep.

On the day of her discharge, I remained cooped up inside my cottage. She knocked on the door around evening.

'If you are done avoiding me, can we talk?' she said when I opened the door.

'I've not been ... come in', I smiled weakly. She was in a pair of jeans and a t-shirt that said 'Come Undone'.

I led her to my study, the tidiest part of my home.

'I have something for you', I said and left the study.

'While you are at it, get me a cup of coffee', she called out.

I came back with a box. 'The coffee is brewing. This is for you. It's ... it's Alice's.' I had gently hand-washed and dried Alice's blue frock.

Pammi ran a hand over the fabric. Her mouth twitched. 'I think you should keep it', she whispered. 'Alice would want that ... yes. I saw you ... you know.'

I looked at her questioningly.

'I saw you when Alice visited me before ... before ... we went into the lake. You watched us as I cut her hair. I don't know the explanation for all this. But these are facts. I also heard you when Alice wouldn't let go of me underwater. I heard your promise to her ... ' Pammi looked at me and I could not meet her eyes.

'I ... I'll get the coffee', I said and got up.

'No, it's fine. I have to leave ... it's a long drive back to Bengaluru.'

'Yes, of course. Well, take care and if you need ... ' I could not complete the sentence. Pammi's lips were on mine.

'I'm sorry Pammi ... I can't', I whispered, although I clung to her. 'I just can't.'

Pammi did not reply. She let go after a couple of minutes.

'It's okay', she said, blowing her nose into a tissue. 'I know you can't have social contact with your patients ... even your ex-patients. I read the ethics guidelines. Every word. To see if there is some option ... '

I did not reply. It felt as if someone was thrusting a stone inside my throat. I ached for her.

'After all we've been through ... I don't think a 356 page manual can come between us', Pammi smiled, trying hard to compose herself. 'I know we will be together. I know it ... just the way I knew about Alice.'

I could not find my voice. I was shattering inside.

'So I won't say bye. I'll ... I'll see you soon.' With a wave she was gone.

I staggered on the porch—the weight of her absence already crushing me. I flopped to the ground and sat still as everything inside me writhed in a pain I did not understand.

I don't know for how long I sat that way. I stirred when someone called my name. It was Nagraj. He gave me a hand and pulled me to my feet.

I did not have to explain anything to him. He knew. 'Man always has options', he said.

True. I could quit my job this instant and go to Pammi. Or I could trust time to take me to her. Trust our love for each other. Trust the power that brought Pammi and Alice to me.

It was time to go watch the deer.

# ACKNOWLEDGEMENTS

I have a tight knot of family and friends who are unconditional in their support and unlimited in their affection. To them, thank you is a very small and insignificant word. Even so, thank you for being there.

From the publishing world, my gratitude goes to the CinnamonTeal Publishing team who are dedicated, passionate, professional and above all, honest. A special mention to this team for the excellent book-cover design.

I am indebted to Neha Potdar, editor—her precise, insightful and uncompromising inputs strengthened the manuscript to a very large extent.

I am most grateful to Rubina Ramesh for being a pillar to many authors like me—you are amazing, Ruby.

Finally, to my Kunal—you are most extraordinary.

# ABOUT THE AUTHOR

Sumana Khan was born and raised in Bangalore where she pursued a career as an IT consultant. She currently lives in the UK and is a full-time writer and student. She holds a Master of Letters in Creative Writing from University of Glasgow and is pursuing her M.Sc. in Psychology. Her website is http://www.sumanakhan.com. ENCOUNTERS is her second book.